***The sight of Laurie brought his pulse
skidding to a halt.***

No matter how many times he saw her picture, he
never got over the wonder of her beauty—the thick
chestnut-colored hair, the dare-you curve of her
smile, the sparkle in her eyes.

This time, though, the photographer hadn't done her
justice. He'd caught Laurie in a moment of stunned
disbelief, one hand held up, futilely trying to shield
the baby in her arms.

She'd been too slow. The baby was in perfect
focus—round-faced, smiling, with a halo of soft
brown curls and blue, blue eyes sparkling with pure
devilment. Adams's eyes, Harlan Patrick thought at
once. Unmistakably Adams' family eyes.

The suspicion that had been nagging him was all
but confirmed.

Laurie Jensen had had his baby.

Dear Reader,

Hold on to your hats, because this month Special Edition has a lineup of romances that you won't soon forget!

We start off with an extraordinary story by #1 *New York Times* bestselling author Nora Roberts. *The Perfect Neighbor* is the eleventh installment of her popular THE MACGREGORS series and spotlights a brooding loner who becomes captivated by his vivacious neighbor.

And the fun is just beginning! *Dream Bride* by Susan Mallery launches her enchanting duet, BRIDES OF BRADLEY HOUSE, about a family legend which has two sisters dreaming about the men they are destined to marry. The first book in the series is also this month's THAT SPECIAL WOMAN! title. Look for the second story, *Dream Groom*, this May.

Next, Christine Rimmer returns with a tale about a single mom who develops a dangerous attraction to a former heartbreaker in *Husband in Training*.

Also don't miss the continuing saga of Sherryl Woods's popular AND BABY MAKES THREE: THE NEXT GENERATION. The latest book in the series, *The Cowboy and his Wayward Bride,* features a hardheaded rancher who will do just about anything to claim the feisty mother of his infant daughter! And Arlene James has written a stirring love story about a sweet young virgin who has every intention of tempting the ornery, much-older rancher down the wedding aisle in *Marrying an Older Man*.

Finally this month, *A Hero at Heart* by Ann Howard White features an emotional reunion romance between an honorable hero and the gentle beauty he's returned for.

I hope you enjoy this book, and each and every novel to come!

Sincerely,

Karen Taylor Richman
Senior Editor

Please address questions and book requests to:
Silhouette Reader Service
U.S.: 3010 Walden Ave., P.O. Box 1325, Buffalo, NY 14269
Canadian: P.O. Box 609, Fort Erie, Ont. L2A 5X3

SHERRYL WOODS

THE COWBOY AND HIS WAYWARD BRIDE

Silhouette®

SPECIAL ▼ EDITION®

Published by Silhouette Books

America's Publisher of Contemporary Romance

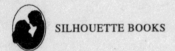 SILHOUETTE BOOKS

ISBN 0-373-24234-4

THE COWBOY AND HIS WAYWARD BRIDE

Copyright © 1999 by Sherryl Woods

Printed in U.S.A.

SHERRYL WOODS

whether she's living in California, Florida or Virginia, Sherryl Woods always makes her home by the sea. A walk on the beach, the sound of waves, the smell of the salt air, all provide inspiration for this writer of more than sixty romance and mystery novels. Sherryl hopes you're enjoying these latest entries in the AND BABY MAKES THREE series for Silhouette Special Edition. You can write to Sherryl, or—from April through December—stop by and meet her at her bookstore, Potomac Sunrise, 308 Washington Avenue, Colonial Beach, VA 22443.

ADAMS FAMILY TREE

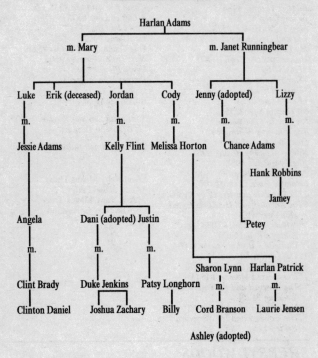

Chapter One

Pure, gut-deep exhaustion had settled over country-music superstar Laurie Jensen weeks earlier, and now it seemed she was walking around in a haze from dawn to dusk. A new baby who didn't know the meaning of a full night's sleep, a concert tour, publicity demands and the burden of keeping a secret from the one person in the world with whom she had always been totally, brutally honest—all of it had combined to take a terrible emotional toll.

She sat in her fancy dressing room long after her concert had ended and the fans had drifted away. With the sleeping baby nestled in her arms, her own eyes drifting shut, she relished the momentary silence, welcoming it just as she had the applause earlier.

Bliss, she thought. The quiet was absolute bliss. Of course, it didn't last.

"Laurie, you ready?" her assistant called out in a hushed tone with an accompanying rap on the door. "The limo's outside to take us back to the hotel."

Even the soft tap and whispered reminder were enough noise to wake the always restless baby, who began to fuss, then settled into a full-throated yowling that gave Laurie a splitting headache.

"Shh, sweetheart. Everything's okay. Mama's here," she soothed, gathering up her purse and easing toward the door.

As the baby quieted and finally began to gurgle contentedly, Laurie did a quick survey of the room to be sure she'd left nothing behind, thankful once again for Val's efficiency. Her assistant handled everything from toting diaper bags to making complex travel arrangements with total aplomb. She'd even been known to tuck Amy Lynn into the crook of her arm and feed her while answering Laurie's fan mail with her free hand.

Often, observing her whirlwind assistant at work, Laurie wished she were half so competent, even a quarter so adept with the multiple demands facing her. There were times—and tonight was one of them—when she felt thoroughly overwhelmed, when she wanted nothing more than to run straight back to Texas and into Harlan Patrick's waiting arms. Assuming he was still waiting for her after all this time and after she'd made it clear that her singing career was what she wanted most in this world.

What was wrong with her? Was she completely out of her mind trying to tackle the demands of motherhood and a singing career all on her own? Especially when she knew with absolute certainty that the baby's father would have flown to her side in a heartbeat if only she'd told him about Amy Lynn?

But that was the trouble, of course. Harlan Patrick Adams would have taken the news that he was a daddy as reason enough to demand that she marry him at once, return to Los Piños, Texas, and be a rancher's wife. There would have been no ifs, ands or buts about it.

She'd known the man since she was in kindergarten. She knew how he operated. A bulldozer did gentle nudging by comparison. Oh, she knew Harlan Patrick, all right. They'd exchanged birthday presents at five, their first awkward dance at thirteen, their first real kiss at fifteen.

Harlan Patrick had flirted with typical Adams abandon with every girl in town, but there'd never been a doubt in anyone's mind that Laurie was the one he loved. With single-minded determination, he'd been asking her to marry him for years now. And she'd been saying no, while practically everyone in the universe told her she'd lost her mind.

Unlike the music business, Harlan Patrick Adams and his love were a sure thing, her mother had told her repeatedly. His family was the richest and most powerful in Los Piños, practically in all of Texas. He could give her stability, the kind of rock-solid future most women dreamed of, the kind her mother had always craved.

Unfortunately, Laurie's dreams tended toward a world that no one, not even an Adams, could guarantee. From the time she'd learned the words to an old Patsy Cline hit, she'd wanted to be a country-music sensation. God had blessed her with the voice for it. Whether it was the church choir or the school chorus, Laurie had always been the star soloist. The applause had been wonderful, but she would have sung for the sheer joy of it. And maybe, at one time, she would have been content with that.

But over the years Harlan Patrick had unwittingly fed her obsession by seeing to it that she saw concerts by every country superstar who appeared anywhere in Texas. He'd even wrangled a backstage meeting with a few. Laurie had discovered her destiny.

Somehow, though, he'd never taken seriously her desire to be up there on the stage, earning her own applause. For him, the gestures had been an indulgence. For her, they had been an inspiration. He'd thought time, a little coaxing and a few breath-stealing kisses would change her mind. She'd found his inability to recognize and accept her dream more annoying than her mom's.

After all, Mary Jensen had had a tough life. She was practical to the very core. Harlan Patrick, however, was supposed to be Laurie's soul mate, the man in whom she'd confided her hopes and dreams all her life. The discovery that he'd merely been indulging what he called "her little fantasies" had brought on one of the most heated fights they'd ever had.

Why hadn't he been able to understand that singing was simply something she had to do with the gift God had given her? He'd let her—*let her,* she thought indignantly—sing in the neighboring towns if that's what she wanted, but Nashville had been out of the question. His ultimatum had been phrased in a generous, condescending tone that had set her teeth on edge. As if the decision were his to make, she'd thought as she turned on her heel and walked out of his life for good.

In one way she was grateful. It had made it easier to say goodbye, to head for Nashville without looking back. She'd dug in her heels, too, even when the going had been tough and she'd been waiting tables to make ends meet. Knowing that he'd welcome her back with an I-told-you-so smile had driven her to stay the course.

It had been two long, lonely years before she'd been discovered by her agent, but then things had happened so quickly it had left her reeling. She'd captured the Horizon Award for up-and-coming stars with her first album, a Grammy and a CMA Award with her second. She'd gone from a show-starter for the superstars to a concert tour of her own that had broken box-office records. In no time, it seemed, every single debuted at the top of the charts and every album went gold.

Only then, with rave reviews and money in her pocket, had she gone back to Los Piños. It was the only time she'd seen Harlan Patrick in the five years since she'd left. She was home just long enough to discover that the chemistry between them was as explosive as ever and that he was every bit as bull-headed as he'd been the day she walked out. He'd actually thought that she'd be ready to walk away from it all now that she'd proved to herself she could do it, as if it had been some cute little game she'd been playing. The man could infuriate her faster than anyone else on earth.

Then, just a few weeks after their reunion, she'd discovered she was pregnant. From that moment on, all she'd been able to think about was keeping the baby a secret from Harlan Patrick. She'd been able to walk away from him not just once, but twice. Could she do it again, especially with a baby in the picture? She wasn't sure she'd have the strength or even the will.

For the first few months of her pregnancy, it had been simple enough to avoid his calls and keep the secret. She was either in Nashville or on the road and she was extremely careful that no one—not even the very discreet Val—had any idea she was going to have a child. Val knew only that she had no desire to speak to one Harlan Patrick Adams, which pretty much assured that there wasn't a chance in hell he'd get through to her. Eventually he'd gotten the message and given up. Not even Harlan Patrick was stubborn beyond all reason. Nor was he a masochist. It hadn't taken all that long for the Adams pride to kick in and assure her of a re-prieve from his pestering.

When Laurie could no longer disguise her expanding waistline, she had scheduled five months in seclusion at her home on the outskirts of Nashville. She'd let Val and no one else in on the secret and let her assistant run interference.

"She's working on songs for her next album," Val had told any and all callers, including Laurie's agent. That had kept him, if not the media, satisfied.

Now she had Amy Lynn to remember her childhood sweetheart by, and it was both the most miraculous blessing on earth and a painful reminder of what might have been. When she thought of how Harlan Patrick would have adored their precious child, she hated herself for keeping silent. And yet, what choice had she had?

None, she assured herself. Handsome as sin, but stubborn as a mule, Harlan Patrick had given her none. The man didn't know the meaning of *compromise*. He'd made it impossible for her to do anything other than exactly what she had done.

After Amy Lynn's birth, she had scheduled recording sessions for the next two months. There'd been a short break, barely long enough for her to catch her breath while the album had been rushed to market, followed by the grueling pace of a concert tour set to coincide with the album's release.

By then, those closest to her knew about the baby, but they'd all been sworn to secrecy and they had united to protect both Laurie and the baby from the glare of the spotlight. It couldn't last forever, but it had to last long enough that Harlan Patrick wouldn't connect her child with that last visit to Los Piños.

It meant sneaking in and out of concert halls and

clubs, using hotel back doors and heavily tinted limo windows, but the worst of it was over. One more month, mostly in small towns and out-of-the-way clubs to which she owed a debt, and they'd be home again. She could drop out of sight completely there, live in seclusion with her daughter. Just thinking of it was enough to have her sighing with relief.

They were halfway down the hall when Val muttered a curse. "I left that package of autographed pictures in the office. Wait for me at the back door, and I'll check the alley before you go out."

It was an established routine. When Laurie had the baby with her, Val always preceded her to make sure the coast was clear, that there were no paparazzi or overly zealous fans lurking in the shadows. Sometimes it was Val who carried Amy Lynn tucked in her arms as if the baby were her own.

Tonight, though, Laurie was thinking only of crawling into the back of the limo, resting her aching head against the smooth-as-butter leather and catching a ten-minute nap on the way back to the hotel. That was how bad it had gotten. Even ten minutes of uninterrupted sleep sounded heavenly.

She was so anxious to reach the car and settle in that she opened the door of the auditorium without waiting for Val. The instant she did, a photographer's flashbulb exploded in her face. Panic had her whirling to shield the baby, but she knew in her heart it was too late. The man had had a clear shot in that instant before she'd been aware of his presence and time to click off a few more shots while she'd been temporarily blinded by the first brilliant flash of light.

"Oh, God, no," she murmured, imagining the picture splashed across the front of every tabloid in the country. Tears slid down her cheeks even as Val exited the building, saw what was happening and took off after the photographer with fire in her eyes.

To Laurie's relief, Val caught him at the end of the alley, but all of her pleading and cajoling could not make him relinquish the prized roll of film. Nor could the swift kick she aimed at his shin or the knee she tried to place deftly in his groin, but Laurie had to admire her courage in trying. She vowed to give the woman a raise for going way above the call of duty, even if her efforts had failed.

Defeated, Val returned to the limo. "I'm sorry," she whispered. "I should have checked the alley."

"It's not your fault," Laurie reassured her wearily. "I should have waited. I was just so tired."

"Maybe he was just some local guy and the picture won't make it beyond here," Val suggested hopefully.

"Ever heard of wire services?" Laurie inquired, wishing she could believe Val, but knowing that she was doomed. Harlan Patrick was going to see the picture. Sooner or later someone would bring it to his attention, and then, no matter what conclusion he reached when he saw it, it was going to rip his heart in two.

Then, she thought with a sinking sensation in the pit of her stomach, all hell was going to break loose. It was just a matter of time.

* * *

"I say we buy up all the copies in town and burn them," Sharon Lynn said vehemently, tossing the offending tabloid onto her parents' kitchen table. "If Harlan Patrick sees this, he's going to freak out."

This was a half-page picture of country-music superstar Laurie Jensen with "Her Secret Love Child."

"He's finally over her," Sharon Lynn said of her brother. "He's not even playing her songs on the new jukebox down at Dolan's anymore."

"No, now he plays them on that boom box he carries with him everywhere he goes," her mother said. "We have to show it to him. Maybe this will finally close that chapter in his life. He'll have to move on once he sees she has a child."

Harlan Patrick stood outside the kitchen door and listened to the whole conversation. His stomach had clenched and his hand had stilled on the screen door the instant he'd realized the topic. The merest mention of Laurie was all it took to get his heart to thudding dully and his forehead to break out in a cold sweat.

How the hell was he supposed to get over Laurie when she was a part of him, as vital to him as breathing? Losing her had made him question everything, every choice he'd made, even his commitment to the family ranch. There were times when the weight of the family's expectations and his sense of his own destiny almost combined to crush him.

With his grandfather in his eighties and his father, Cody, getting older, the fate of White Pines was all but his. Ranching was in his blood; it defined who he was, but that didn't make it any less of a burden at times. Day in, day out, 365 days a year, the demands were unceasing. The damned ranch was what stood between him and Laurie, and yet, when the chips had been down, the ranch was what he'd chosen, just as surely as she'd chosen her music over him.

His heritage over his heart. It was pitiful enough to be the heartbreaking theme of a country-music megahit. He was surprised Laurie hadn't written it herself. She'd turned everything else they'd shared into top-ten hits. There was something downright eerie and irritating about hearing his life played out on the radio.

Thinking back, he realized that maybe he'd made the decisions he had because he hadn't believed for a minute that she'd really leave. Despite repeated warnings from his sister, his cousin Justin, his grandfather, just about everyone, he'd trusted that their love was stronger than anything else on earth. By the time he'd recognized his mistake, it was too late. Laurie had been gone and with her, his soul.

Ironically he'd gotten another chance a little over a year ago, but his pride had kicked in with a vengeance and he'd watched her run out on him all over again. Pride, as his granddaddy had told him more than once, made a mighty cold bedmate. Even knowing the truth of that, he still hadn't been able to make himself go after her. He'd called for a while, but when those calls hadn't been returned, he'd cursed her every which way and given up.

Okay, so he was a damned fool. He admitted it. She'd made things clear enough the last time he'd seen her. She'd told him flat out that she still loved him, just not enough to come home and be his wife. He'd accepted her decision. What choice did he have? He couldn't go chasing halfway around the world to be by her side, could he? What was he supposed to do? Run White Pines long-distance?

But he hadn't forgotten about her, not for a single second. Now she had a child? He didn't believe it, couldn't believe that some other man had shared her bed, not when she'd so fiercely declared that she was still in love with him. Theirs simply wasn't the kind of love that died overnight, no matter how badly they'd mistreated each other. No one had replaced her in his heart or even in his bed. He'd managed to convince himself that she'd do the same. Apparently that was just one on a whole long list of delusions he'd held about Laurie.

He yanked open the screen door, then let it slam behind him as he stared into two shocked, guilty faces. "Let me see it," he demanded, his voice deadly calm.

Sharon Lynn moved between him and the table, blocking his view of the paper. "Forget about it," she said. "Forget about her."

He watched as her sense of indignation and family loyalty kicked in and loved her for it. His big sister had a mile-wide protective streak. All of the Adamses did.

"Laurie Jensen isn't worth one more second of

your time," Sharon Lynn declared. "She's never been any good for you, and this proves it."

"I know what you're trying to do, sis, but you and I both know that Laurie is the only woman for me."

Sharon Lynn blushed. "Okay, I'm sorry. It just makes me so mad the way she keeps walking out on you."

He decided not to remind her that that was only half of the story. The first time Laurie had gone, Sharon Lynn had actually taken her side, accused him of being a short-sighted jerk for not going after her, for not trying harder to become a part of her new life, maybe using his business degree to become her manager or something. When Laurie had gone this last time, Sharon Lynn had positioned herself staunchly behind him. Rarely did a kind word about Laurie cross her lips. The rest of his family tried never to mention her at all.

He scowled at Sharon Lynn. "Just hand over the paper, okay?"

His sister wasn't quite finished. Once she got wound up, it was impossible to slow her down. She gave him defiant look. "You have to forget about her, Harlan Patrick. Move on. There are a zillion women in Texas who'd love to be with you. Pick one of them, one who'll treat you right instead of running out on everything you have to offer."

"Easier said than done," he said.

He ought to know. He'd cut a wide swath through the available women in three or four counties after Laurie had left the first time. He hadn't had more than a date or two with any of them then and he hadn't bothered to call even one of them after Laurie had left this last time. He'd accepted the possibility that no one would ever measure up.

"Sis, I appreciate your loyalty. I really do," he assured her, then glared. "Now let me see the blasted paper, unless you'd prefer to have me drive all the way into town to pick one up. Do you want me to be standing in the supermarket with half the town gawking at me when I read it? That ought to keep the gossips busy for a while."

His mother, who'd been letting the two of them battle it out up until now, sighed. "Let him see it, Sharon Lynn. The horse is out of the barn anyway."

His sister handed him the paper with obvious reluctance. The front page was folded in two. He opened it slowly, regretting that he had even his mother and sister as his audience.

The sight of Laurie, all done up in her fancy, rhinestone-studded cowgirl stage costume, brought his pulse skidding to a halt. No matter how many times he saw her picture, he never got over the wonder of her beauty—the thick chestnut-colored hair, the dare-you curve of her smile, the sparkle in her eyes. Despite the fancy getup, there was no artifice about her. She didn't need a lot of makeup to enhance what nature had given her.

He'd pretty much stopped looking at these rags, because the sight of her always had the same effect and he figured sooner or later it was going to turn deadly. How many times could a man's heart grind to a halt before it stopped pumping altogether?

This time, though, the photographer hadn't done her justice. There was no glint in her eyes, no smile on her lips. He'd caught her in an instant of stunned disbelief, one hand held up, futilely trying to block the lens, while she turned to try to shield the baby in her arms.

She'd been too slow. The baby was in perfect focus, round faced, smiling, with a halo of soft brown curls and blue, blue eyes sparkling with pure devilment. Adams eyes, Harlan Patrick thought at once, unmistakably Adams eyes. There was a whole mantle full of baby pictures just like this up at Grandpa Harlan's. He was surprised his mother and Sharon Lynn hadn't guessed the truth—but then they hadn't known about that last meeting—the one where he lost his head and made love to her one last time.

This time it wasn't love or even lust that kicked his pulse into overdrive. It was fury. The suspicion that had been nagging at him from the moment he'd heard his mother and Sharon Lynn talking was all but confirmed. Laurie Jensen had had his baby and kept it from him. Betrayal cut through him like a lance. He was surprised he wasn't bleeding from the wound.

In less than an instant, fury was replaced by icy resolve. He whirled around and without a word went out the way he'd come in, slamming the door behind him, the tabloid crushed in his hand.

"Oh, my God," Sharon Lynn murmured. "Did you see his face?"

"I saw," his mother said, racing out the door after him. "Harlan Patrick, get back here!"

He ignored the command and headed straight for his pickup. A half hour later he was at the airstrip with Uncle Jordan's corporate jet fired up and waiting for him.

He was going after Laurie Jensen and his baby and when he found them, there was going to be hell to pay.

Chapter Two

Laurie had been heartsick ever since her manager had shown her the tabloid a week after that fateful night outside a Kansas concert hall. From that moment on she had prayed over and over that Harlan Patrick would never see it. Whether he recognized the baby as his or not, the picture was going to break his heart. She'd vowed the last time she'd seen him not to ever do anything to hurt him again. As it was, she'd broken his heart more times than she could count.

She'd tried to prepare for the possibility that her prayers wouldn't be heard. She'd warned everyone in her agent's office that her schedule was not to be given to anyone, no matter what name they gave, no matter what ruse they used. She had described

Harlan Patrick to Nick's secretary from his thick, sun-streaked hair, to his laser blue eyes and angled cheekbones.

"And you *don't* want this man to find you?" the woman had said incredulously. "Are you nuts?"

"There are those who'd say I am," she agreed. "And, Ruby, let me know the instant he shows up, okay? I need to know what kind of mood he's in."

"Fit to be tied would be my guess," Ruby said bluntly. "Can't say I blame him, either. It's a hell of a way to find out you're a daddy."

"Ruby," Laurie protested.

"Okay, okay, I'm just the hired help around here. You don't want the man to find you, I'll make sure the man doesn't find you, at least not with any help from me. Just don't forget, honey, you're the kind of woman who tends to make news, especially in this business. *Entertainment Tonight*'s scheduled to shoot that club date in Montana. It's way too late to back out. Nick would have a cow. He worked like crazy to get it set up."

"It won't matter. By the time it airs, I'll be on the road again. With any sort of luck at all, Harlan Patrick will be one step behind me."

"Maybe you ought to slow down and let him catch up," Ruby suggested one more time. "Have it out and get it over with. Hiding's no good, not in your profession. This was bound to happen sooner or later. And, forgive me for saying it, but that little girl of yours has a right to know her daddy. This plan of yours to keep 'em apart seems a tad selfish to me."

Laurie winced. Ruby was young, but she had terrific common sense and a mile-wide streak of decency. A part of Laurie wanted to follow her advice, but another part wasn't at all sure she could cope with one more battle with Harlan Patrick, not with the stakes as high as they were.

"I know," Laurie conceded. "But I can't deal with him yet. I just can't. You'll see what I mean if he shows up there. It's like trying to talk sense with a bulldozer that's rattling toward you in first gear."

Of course, she consoled herself, there was always the outside chance that Harlan Patrick had never even seen the tabloid. Maybe he hadn't been anywhere near a supermarket checkout stand. Maybe the entire shipment to Los Piños had been lost in transit. Maybe the delivery truck had caught fire. Maybe...

Dammit, she had to know. She had to find out if he'd seen it and what his reaction had been. She had to be prepared, in case he was coming after her. For all of her attempts to cover her tracks, she knew Ruby was right. If Harlan Patrick wanted to find her badly enough, he could. Ruby and Nick could only stall him for so long. Any private eye worth his license could pinpoint her location quicker than that photographer had snapped her picture. The only real question was whether Harlan Patrick was furious enough to come chasing after her or so hurt he'd written her off once and for all. If he'd recognized that baby as his, she was pretty sure which it would be. He'd be mowing down any obstacle in his path to get to her.

She could call her mother, but her mom almost never crossed paths with Harlan Patrick's family. She could call Sharon Lynn, but after this last visit, Harlan Patrick's protective older sister had all but written her off. Sharon Lynn had told her more than once that she was a selfish fool for running off and leaving the best man in the whole state of Texas pining after her. His parents had never echoed the same sentiments in so many words, but they clearly hadn't been her biggest fans. When she'd come back this last time, they'd regarded her with suspicion at worst, caution at best. The attitude had hurt, because once they'd considered her another daughter.

That left his grandfather. Harlan Adams was a wise man, a fair man. He'd protect his family with his dying breath, but he also had the ability to see that there was more than one side to most stories. He'd always treated Laurie with kindness, and there'd been no judgment in his eyes when she'd left yet again, only sorrow. He would tell her what she needed to know and he wouldn't pull any punches.

It took her most of the day to work up the courage to call White Pines. She told herself it was because she wasn't likely to find Harlan Adams at home much before nightfall. Despite his age, he still worked the ranch as best he could. And when his aches kept him off a horse, he was busy meddling in everyone's lives.

The truth, though, was that she was scared to hear whatever he had to say, even more afraid that this time he wouldn't be so kind at all if he thought she had betrayed his grandson.

She shouldn't have worried. Either he didn't know about the baby or he'd taken it in stride. At any rate, he greeted her with his usual exuberance.

"Laurie, darlin' girl, how are you? Pretty as ever, I know, because I see your picture in the paper and on TV all the time. You still singing up a storm?"

"I'm busier than ever," she told him. "I'm right in the middle of a concert tour now. I won't be back in Nashville for another month." She figured it wouldn't hurt to reiterate that, in case the conversation was repeated to Harlan Patrick. Maybe he'd stay away from Nashville if he knew she wouldn't be there.

"And you enjoy all this wandering around, instead of taking the time to sit a spell in one place?" Harlan Adams asked.

"Most of the time," she admitted. "It's part of the job."

"Tell me about the next album. You finished it yet?"

"No. I haven't even started. This one's only been out a couple of months now. I probably won't get back into the studio until a few months after I get back to Nashville. It's a good thing, too. I've been scribbling down a few things, but I still haven't settled on the last two songs."

"You still writing them all yourself?"

"Most of them."

"You always had a way with words. I still remember that song you wrote and sang for me when

I turned eighty. Not a dry eye in the place when you were done singing. I knew then you were going to be a superstar.''

"That's more than I knew then."

Silence fell, and it was Harlan who finally broke it when Laurie couldn't find the words she needed.

"So, darlin' girl, you just calling to say hi, or is something on your mind?'' There was a sly, knowing tone to his voice.

Just say it, she instructed herself firmly, then swallowed hard. "Actually, well, I was wondering about Harlan Patrick. He's been on my mind a lot lately.''

"I see."

Clearly he didn't intend to give away a thing without her asking a direct question. "How's he doing?'' she asked finally.

"Still misses you, if that's what you're asking. I suspect he always will. Never seen a man as lovesick as he was from the minute you left town.''

That wasn't what she'd been asking, but in some tiny corner of her heart, she was glad to hear that he hadn't forgotten her. Talk about conflicting emotions. Her life was riddled with them.

"You've seen him in the last couple of days?'' she asked, broaching the subject of his whereabouts cautiously.

Harlan hesitated. "Now that you mention it, his daddy did say that the boy had taken off unexpectedly. Never did mention what it was all about, though. Business, I suppose. You want me to have him call you when he gets back?''

Laurie sighed heavily. She had a feeling there would be no need for that. The timing of his unexplained departure had to be more than coincidence. If she knew Harlan Patrick, she'd be seeing him any day now, as soon as he could get someone to give him her concert itinerary.

"That's okay," she said, then added quietly, "thank you."

"Thanks for what?"

"For not hating me."

"Oh, darlin' girl, I could never hate you," he said, his tone sympathetic. "There was a time when you were practically family. As far as I'm concerned, you're as good as that now."

"But I brought so much pain into Harlan Patrick's life."

"And so much joy, too," he reminded her. "Don't forget that. Sometimes the best you can hope for in life is that it all evens out in the end. You take good care of yourself and come see me next time you're home. I'll get the piano tuned, and we'll have an old-fashioned sing-along. I can't carry a tune worth a hoot, but it'll be fun all the same."

"I will," she promised. "Give Janet my love, too, will you?"

"Of course I will. You take good care of yourself, Laurie. Don't forget all the folks back here who love you."

As if I could, she thought, but didn't say. "Goodbye, Grandpa Harlan. I miss you."

Only after she'd hung up did she realize there were tears streaming down her cheeks. For the first time in more than six years, she realized just how much she missed home. And when she thought of it, she didn't remember the little house in which she'd grown up, didn't even think of her mother, though she loved her dearly. No, she remembered White Pines and the close-knit Adamses, who back then had been more than willing to accept her as one of their own.

And she remembered Amy Lynn's daddy and the way she'd always loved him.

He might as well have been traveling in a foreign country, Harlan Patrick thought on his first day in Nashville. He'd taken off without thinking, without the slightest clue of how to go about tracing a woman who didn't want to be found.

On the flight, which he'd piloted himself, he'd had plenty of time to try to formulate a plan, but images of Laurie and that baby had pretty much wiped out logic. All he'd been able to feel was some sort of blind rage. Aside from a friendly tussle or two with his cousins growing up, he wasn't prone to violence, but for the first time in his life he felt himself capable of it. Not that he'd have laid a hand on Laurie, but he couldn't swear that her furniture would be safe. Smashing a few vases and chairs might improve his mood considerably.

Then again, it probably wouldn't. Satisfaction probably couldn't be had that easily.

After landing, he rented a car and drove into downtown. He found a hotel smack in the center of things and dragged out a phone book. It was then that he realized just how little he really knew about Laurie's life in the past few years. An awful lot of it had been played out in public, of course, but that wasn't the part that would help him now.

"Well, damn," he muttered staring at the Yellow Pages and trying to figure out which talent representative or which recording studio to call. He couldn't even remember which record label produced her albums, even though he had CDs of every single one of them. It was hard enough listening to her songs without learning every little detail of the life that had stolen her from him.

He plucked a scrap of paper out of his pocket and glanced at the number, then dialed her house first, though he recognized it was a long shot. She was on the road and she'd told him that she'd never gotten around to hiring a housekeeper because she wasn't comfortable with somebody else doing cleaning and cooking she was perfectly capable of doing for herself.

When no one answered at the house, he searched his memory for some offhand reference she'd made to the new people in her life. Unfortunately, though, the few days they'd had together just over a year ago hadn't been spent doing a lot of talking, at least not about the things that hadn't mattered. That baby was living evidence that they'd spent most of the time in bed, remembering just how good it felt to be in each other's arms.

"Okay, Harlan Patrick, think," he muttered under his breath.

For all of its skyscrapers and new construction,

Nashville was still a small Southern town in some ways. Surely the music industry was tight-knit enough that everyone would know everybody else's business. He picked a talent agency at random and dialed.

"Hi, sweetheart," he said to the drawling woman who answered. There was enough sugary sweetness in her voice to make him feel right at home with a little flirting. He had her laughing in a matter of seconds.

"You are sooo bad," she said in response to his teasing. "Now, tell me what I can do for you."

"Actually I've got some business to do with Laurie Jensen. Any idea how I can get in touch with her?"

"Laurie Jensen?" she repeated, her voice a degree or two cooler. "I'm sorry. We don't represent Miss Jensen."

"Could you tell me who does?"

"What kind of business did you say you were in?" she asked. This time her tone was downright chilly.

"I didn't, darlin', but it's an ad campaign. We were hoping to get her to do the spots for us."

"I see," she said. "Well, maybe you ought to have your ad agency contact her people. That's the way it works."

Harlan Patrick tried to hold on to his patience. "Don't you see, sugar, that's the problem. I don't know her people."

"Any reputable ad agency will," she said, and hung up in his ear.

Harlan Patrick stared at the phone, stunned. Then he sighed ruefully. Obviously he wasn't the first person to try a ruse to get to a Nashville superstar. He resigned himself to an afternoon spent working his way through the phone listings.

He didn't waste time trying to wrangle information from unwilling receptionists. The minute he discovered the agency didn't represent Laurie, he moved on to the next. It was after six when he finally struck paydirt—or thought he had.

"Nick Sanducci's office."

"Yes. I'm trying to arrange a booking for Laurie Jensen. Can you help me?"

"Who are you with, sir?"

"Does Mr. Sanducci represent Ms. Jensen?"

"He does, but—"

"Thank you." He hung up and grabbed his hat. Clutching the page from the phone book and scribbled directions from the hotel desk clerk, he drove to a quiet street that looked more residential than commercial. A block or so from the address for Sanducci's office, he noted the discreet signs on the lawns of modest-sized homes that appeared to have been built around the turn of the century. Law offices, talent agencies, even a recording studio had been tucked away here before skyscrapers had lured most of the business into downtown.

Harlan Patrick pulled into a circular driveway just as a fancy sports car shot out the other side. One car remained in front of the house, a minivan with a child's seat in the back and toys scattered on the floor. He doubted it belonged to Mr. Nick Sanducci.

He strolled through the front door and wandered into a reception room that had obviously once been the house's living room. The walls were decorated with gold records and photos of a half dozen of the hottest names in country music, including a blowup of Laurie that could make a man's knees weak. That wall of photos and records was the only testament to the nature of Mr. Sanducci's business, however.

Harlan Patrick had to admit the man had excellent taste. The place was crammed with exquisite, expensive antiques. There were some just as valuable up in Grandpa Harlan's attic, where they'd been stored after Janet had gone through and turned White Pines from a hands-off showplace into a home.

The reception desk was neat as a pin and, with no one seated at the chair behind it, more temptation than he could resist. He edged a little closer, noting that the desk belonged to one Ruby Steel, according to the nameplate that was half-buried in a stack of papers.

He surveyed the rest of the desk with interest. That big old Rolodex probably had phone numbers on it that could do him a whole lot of good. And that bulging desk calendar probably contained all sorts of concert dates, including Laurie's.

He was about to make a grab for it when a lazy, sultry voice inquired with just a touch of frost, "Can I help you?"

He turned slowly and offered the sort of grin that had gotten him out of many a scrape over the years, at least if there was a female involved. Ruby was

young enough to look susceptible, but her frown
never wavered. Obviously a woman who took her
last name—Steel—to heart.

"Hey, darlin', I was just wondering where you'd
gone off to."

"And you thought you'd find me under the
desk?" She gave him a thorough once-over that
could have served her well at a police lineup. "Let
me guess. You're the one who called wanting to
book Laurie Jensen."

He could have lied, probably should have, but
something told him the truth would get him what he
needed a whole lot faster.

"You've got a good ear for voices, sugar."

"And I've got the good sense not to go giving
out information to strangers," she said in a tone that
warned him not to waste his time trying to wheedle
anything out of her.

Harlan Patrick was undaunted. He pretended he
hadn't been close enough to discover the nameplate
and asked, "What's your name, sugar?"

"My name's Ruby, cowboy, and there's no need
telling me yours, because it doesn't matter. I can't
help you."

His gaze narrowed at that. Something told him
that Laurie had given this woman very clear and
specific instructions where he was concerned.

"Now, why is that? Aren't you in the business of
getting work for your clients?"

"Nick is. My job is protecting them."

"Then maybe I ought to talk to Nick."

"You can't. He's gone."

The fancy sports car, Harlan Patrick concluded. "When will he be back?"

"Hard to say. Nick's unpredictable."

"Tonight?"

"I doubt it."

"Tomorrow morning?"

"Possibly. Then again, he could get a call from one of his clients and have to take off in the middle of the night."

Harlan Patrick hid a grin. Ruby was tough, all right. "How often does that happen?"

"You'd be surprised."

"I don't suppose you'd like to go out for a drink?"

She waved her left hand under his nose. A wedding ring and diamond flashed past. "I don't think so, cowboy. And you could get me drunk as a skunk and I still wouldn't tell you how to find Laurie."

"Because she told you not to," he guessed aloud.

Ruby hesitated for just an instant, then nodded. "Because she told me not to and because I protect the privacy of all our clients. I value their trust."

"What if I told you I was her old childhood sweetheart?"

"I'd ask how come she left you behind if you were all that special."

The barb hit its mark. "Now, darlin', that is the sixty-four-thousand-dollar question." He regarded her thoughtfully. "You know, don't you?"

For the first time, little Miss Ruby squirmed. "Know what?"

"That I'm the daddy of that baby of hers."

"I don't know any such thing," she retorted, but there was a telltale flush in her cheeks.

He kept right on. "And you don't believe that a daddy should be separated from his child, do you, Ruby?" He recalled the baby seat in the van outside. "You're a mama yourself. You disapprove of what Laurie's done to me. I could see it in the way the corners of your mouth turned down when I mentioned that baby."

She ducked her head. "It doesn't matter what I think."

"Because your duty's to Laurie."

Her chin came up, and she shot a defiant look straight at him. "Exactly."

They stood there, facing each other, neither of them saying a word, until finally Harlan Patrick sighed.

"Would it matter if I told you I love her?"

Her expression softened. "It might to me, but I'm not the one who needs convincing, am I?"

He grinned. "No, but you are the one who stands between me and her."

She grinned back. "You are a sneaky, persistent devil—I'll give you that."

Harlan Patrick felt a faint stirring of hope. "Will you help me, Ruby?"

Still smiling, she looked him straight in the eye and said, "No. Now, scoot along out of here, cowboy. I'm closing for the day."

"I'll be back in the morning," he promised, taking the defeat with good grace. Ranting and raving wouldn't work with a woman like Ruby, but he had a hunch that he could wear her down with charm and a few more reminiscences about the old days he'd shared with Laurie.

"Suit yourself, but the answer won't be one bit different tomorrow."

"We'll see," he said, and tipped his hat. "It's been my pleasure, darlin'."

She gave him a stern, no-nonsense look. "I can't imagine why. You look like a man who's all too used to getting his own way."

He winked. "I am. That's why it's fascinating to run into a worthy challenge every now and again."

He slipped out the door before she could respond to that. He drove down the block and parked around the corner. He didn't doubt for an instant that Ruby would be on the phone to Laurie the moment he was out of sight.

And the moment Ruby was gone for the night, he intended to sneak back into the office, punch Redial and discover for himself exactly where Laurie Jensen was holed up with his baby girl.

Chapter Three

Going back into Nick Sanducci's office and checking the phone had been a good idea. Maybe even a great idea, Harlan Patrick thought ruefully. Unfortunately Ruby was either on to him and hadn't used the office phone to call Laurie or had simply made another call after that. He'd managed to slip back into the building easily enough—the locks were downright pitiful—but when he'd pressed the Redial button, a very cranky man had growled hello, then slammed the phone down when Harlan Patrick had been too stunned and disappointed to speak.

His reaction proved what a lousy detective he'd make. Only afterward had he considered all the possible explanations for who that man might have been. It could have been someone answering for

Laurie herself. Or it could have been her agent, Nick Sanducci, he concluded belatedly, regretting his silence. But even if it was the illustrious, high-powered agent, he was clearly in no mood to indulge Harlan Patrick's request for information about Laurie. He resigned himself to waiting for morning and another round with Ruby.

Back in his hotel room after a steak dinner that had tasted like sawdust, he was able to think rationally. He recognized that he ought to be grateful for the delay. In her own way Laurie was every bit as stubborn as he was—to say nothing of unpredictable. She had the financial wherewithal nowadays to simply disappear, taking his daughter with her. Obviously, confronting her when he was ready to commit mayhem was no way to get what he wanted.

Whatever that was, he amended with a sigh. It occurred to him that he ought to figure that much out at least before coming face-to-face with the woman who generally rendered him tongue-tied and weak-kneed.

Did he just want to see his child? Did he want to exact revenge on Laurie for deceiving him? Or did he want what he'd always wanted, to take both of them home with him, to have a family with Laurie Jensen?

One thing for certain—he needed to figure all that out before he blasted his way back into her life. He needed to be seeing things clearly and thinking straight, or she'd waltz right out of his life one more time. Something told him this was their very last chance to get it right.

He spent two frustrating days thinking about Laurie, the baby and their future, while trying to convince Ruby to divulge Laurie's itinerary to him. Nick proved as elusive as a stray calf loose on ten thousand acres of pastureland, but Ruby was mellowing. Harlan Patrick had been plying her with chocolate-covered doughnuts and compliments and he was pretty sure she was weakening. She'd actually tossed a handful of newspaper clippings at him that morning and told him to figure out Laurie's whereabouts for himself.

"You're a clever man. See what you can make of these," she'd challenged.

There was plenty of information to be had in those clippings, bits of rave reviews, comments on her new album's fast rise in the music charts. It was plain that Laurie Jensen was hot news in Nashville. The only trouble was that that news was a day too late to help him find her. By the time Ruby handed over the clippings, even the most recent ones, Laurie was already moving on.

He was back at the agent's office for the third straight day, when a teenager who was working part-time finally took pity on him and slipped him a copy of the concert schedule. He had a feeling Ruby had looked the other way—or maybe even instigated it, but he was careful not to let on what he thought. Ruby plainly felt her integrity was on the line, but just as plainly she felt that Laurie's baby deserved to have a daddy in her life. She'd all but admitted that to him on several occasions.

Clutching the itinerary in his hand, he grabbed his

bag from the hotel and headed for the airport, where once again Jordan's jet was fueled up and waiting. Laurie was scheduled for a stop in Montana, then a hop over to Wyoming, a jog back to Montana, then after a two-day break, the Ohio State Fairgrounds. Columbus was closest, but he didn't want to wait another minute, much less several days. Too much time had been wasted already. He calculated the flying time and figured he could make that first Montana stop in time for her closing set.

An icy calm settled over him as he flew, but as he drove to the country-western bar where she was singing, an old, familiar sense of anticipation began to build. It was doggone irritating that she could still have that effect on him, especially under these circumstances when he very much wanted to wring her neck. His pulse was zipping with lust, not adrenaline.

He found the bar after a few wrong turns. It was bigger than some he'd seen, but smaller than he'd expected a star on the rise to be playing. In fact, the End of the Road back in Garden City had been a step above this place. He found that irksome, too. She could have stayed in Texas and done this well for herself.

Then he recalled what he'd read in one of the clippings, that part of this tour had been arranged to settle old debts to club owners who'd given her a break. Typical of Laurie. She was loyal and generous. If it hadn't been for him, she'd probably have played the End of the Road on this tour as well. If he'd had a lick of sense or any foresight, he'd have had the owner ask and then Laurie could have come to him, instead of the other way around. Of course, because of the baby, she probably wouldn't have set foot near the place. But that was water under the bridge anyway. He was here now, and Laurie was only a hundred yards away or less.

With the bar's front door ajar on the warm night, the sound of her voice washed over him as he walked from the parking lot toward the neon-lit building. She had the kind of voice that made a man think of sin, no matter how innocent the words. It was low and sultry and filled with magic.

How many nights had he lain awake remembering the whisper of that voice in his ear? How many days had he played her albums as he worked around the ranch? Enough that he and most of the hands knew the lyrics of her songs by heart. One daring newcomer, who didn't know their history, had made a suggestive remark about Laurie, only to have Harlan Patrick yank him out of his saddle and scare him half to death before reason kicked in.

Heaven knew, the woman could sing. He grabbed hold of the door and braced himself to enter, reminding himself to stay calm no matter what. Only after he walked inside the bar did he realize that what he'd heard had come from a jukebox, while the impatient audience waited for the second set to begin. Harlan Patrick slipped into the shadows in the back, ordered a beer and waited.

A few minutes later Laurie emerged amid a flash of red, white and blue strobe lights, the beat of the song fast and hard and upbeat. The wall-to-wall crowd was on its feet at once, and the whole place began to rock with the sound of her music and wild applause. She kept up the fever pitch through one song, then two, then a third. Just when Harlan Patrick was sure half the room was going to pass out from the frenzy, she turned the tempo down and had them swaying quietly to a tune so sad and soul weary, he almost shed a tear or two himself.

A cynic might have said she was manipulative. A critic would have said she had the crowd in the palm of her hand. Harlan Patrick simply wondered at the mixed emotions he felt listening to the woman he loved captivate a whole roomful of strangers. He'd had her to himself for so many years. Was that the real problem, that he didn't want to share her with the world? Was it selfishness, as much as cussedness, that had made him refuse to search harder for a compromise?

The thought that possessiveness might be the root of their troubles made him too uncomfortable to stay in the room a moment longer. While the show went on, he slipped out the door and made his way to the club's back entrance, which was also standing open to permit the night's breeze to drift inside the overheated club.

Harlan Patrick had no trouble slipping past the bulky, fiftyish guard. The man was too busy gazing at the woman on stage, his foot tapping to the beat of her song, a smile on his lips and a yearning in his eyes. That was when Harlan Patrick realized that part of Laurie's success was her ability to touch hearts and inspire dreams, even the impossible ones.

The backstage area was cramped, with barely enough room for an office, a storeroom and one remaining room that had to be Laurie's dressing room. He opened the door, saw the tumble of clothes and cosmetics and smiled for the first time in ages. Laurie never had been much for picking up after herself.

It was a no-frills dressing room, with a metal rod for a clothes rack and bare bulbs around a square mirror. The chair in front of the dressing table was molded plastic, but the bouquet of flowers beside the scattered makeup was lavish enough for the biggest superstar.

While he waited, he tidied up, folding this, hanging that on the bare metal rod stuck in an alcove. He lingered over a scrap of lace and prayed to heaven no man had ever seen her wearing it. He'd have to rip his eyes out. Finally he tucked the panties into the suitcase sitting on the floor in the corner and pulled out the room's only other chair—a straight-backed monstrosity with a seat covered in tattered red plastic. He turned it around until he could straddle it and face the door.

He heard the last refrain of the encore die down, then the thunder of applause, then the sound of laughter in the corridor and boots on the hardwood floor outside the door. His pulse thundered as loudly as a summer storm.

The door swung open and there she was, pretty as ever, with her color high and her long, chestnut brown hair mussed and glistening with glints of gold and damp with perspiration. He'd seen her looking just like that after sex, only without so many clothes on.

Her mouth formed a soft "oh" of stunned dismay. The color washed out of her cheeks, and for just an instant he thought she might faint, but Laurie was made of tougher stuff than that. She squared her shoulders and met his gaze evenly.

"Hey, darlin'!" Harlan Patrick said in his friendliest tone. "Surprised to see me?"

Laurie's pulse was racing so fast, she was certain she was only a beat or two shy of a medical emergency. She'd guessed Harlan Patrick would hunt her down—*known* he was coming, thanks to Ruby's warning call—but seeing him here, so at home in her dressing room, had caught her off guard.

How many times had she found him waiting for her just like this in the old days? How many times had she come offstage, giddy with excitement, and rushed into his waiting arms to be twirled around until her head spun? Of course, there was no crooked grin tonight and his arms were crossed along the back of that pitiful chair, not waiting to catch her up in an exuberant hug.

Lordy, he was gorgeous. Under other circumstances her pulse would have been scrambling from pure desire, rather than panic. The Adams genes were the best in Texas, maybe the best on earth. Even travel weary, Harlan Patrick was pure male, from that angled jaw to his broad shoulders and right on down to the tips of his dusty boots. The sensual curve of his mouth was a reminder of deep, hot kisses that could rock her to her soul.

But the look on his face, so cool and neutral and composed, was worrisome. Harlan Patrick's emotions were usually right out there for anyone to see. Only when she looked into his eyes did she detect the fire of complete and total fury. That's when she knew that not only had he seen the tabloid, but he'd also realized that Amy Lynn was his.

That left her with a quandary. She could fold right now and throw herself on his mercy or she could stand up to him the way she'd been doing since their first playground scuffle so many years ago. Her first rule in dealing with him had always been to get the upper hand and hang on for dear life. It was the only way she knew to deal with a steamroller.

"How did you get in here?" she demanded, every bit the haughty superstar.

"Unfortunately for you, the security guard's a fan. He never even noticed me. Be glad I wasn't a stalker, sugar, or you'd be in a heap of trouble."

She had a feeling in his own way, Harlan Patrick was every bit as dangerous as any stranger about now. "I could have the guard in here in a flash if you start stirring up trouble," she threatened. "Nobody gets backstage without a pass, and Chester has a very jittery trigger finger."

"Now, darlin', why would I want to stir up trouble for you?" he asked in a patient tone belied by that hard glint in his eyes.

She refused to be taken in by the deceptively mild question. Skepticism lacing her voice, she asked,

"Then this is purely a social call? You just happened to be in Montana and thought you'd drop by to catch the show? We're just a couple of old friends getting together to catch up?"

"Could be."

"Why don't I believe that for a minute?"

"Guilt, maybe?"

He looked her over so thoroughly, so knowingly, that it took everything in her not to bolt or spill her guts, pouring out the whole story behind her decision to keep Amy Lynn a secret from him. She forced herself to wait him out.

"So, tell me, Laurie," he began eventually, "anything new in your life?"

Oh, he knew, all right, she thought, listening to this cat-and-mouse game of his. She could have strung him along for another minute or two, maybe more, but why bother? Now that he'd found her, they were going to hash this out sooner or later. Hopefully they could get it over with right here in her dressing room. It was a hell of a lot better than having it out at the hotel, where Amy Lynn was already fast asleep with Val watching over her.

She looked him straight in the eye and forced his hand. "Come on, Harlan Patrick, spit it out. You saw the tabloid, didn't you?"

His gaze locked with hers. "I did."

There was that neutral tone again. It was maddening. "And?" she prodded.

"And I want to know why the hell you kept my daughter a secret from me?"

There was the blast of temper she'd been expecting, the confirmation that he'd guessed it all. Laurie didn't bother trying to deny the truth. In fact, she was glad it was finally out in the open. The secret had been weighing her down for months now, ever since the home pregnancy test she'd taken had turned out positive. She hadn't been able to go near Los Piños so her mama could see the baby for fear of Harlan Patrick finding out that she'd deceived him. At last she could put all of that behind her. She told herself she should be grateful, but all she felt was a gut-wrenching sense of fear.

"I made a choice," she told him quietly. "You and I had said our goodbyes. We had finally admitted once and for all that it wouldn't work with me being on the road all the time and you chained to that ranch you love so much. How could I tell you that there was a baby on the way?"

"How could you not tell me?" he countered in that same patient, lethal tone. "Did you think for one second I wouldn't want to know, that I didn't deserve to know?"

"No, of course not, but—"

He was on his feet now, pacing, agitation replacing patience and calm.

"But nothing," he said, whirling on her.

He grabbed her arms, clearly fighting the urge to shake her. With any other man she might have been afraid of the look in his eyes, but she knew Harlan Patrick as well as she knew any human on earth. There wasn't a violent bone in his body. Even now, he had a tight rein on his temper.

Then again, as far as she knew, he'd never been tested like this before.

She looked into his eyes and saw beyond the outrage, saw the genuine hurt and anguish, and that was her undoing. Tears spilled down her cheeks.

"I'm sorry," she whispered. "I'm sorry. I didn't know what else to do."

He regarded her incredulously. "Couldn't you have called me, talked to me? There was a time when we brought all our problems to each other. We could have worked something out."

"We'd said our goodbyes," she repeated. "I couldn't go stirring things up again, not when there were no easy answers. It wouldn't have been fair."

"Fair?" he all but shouted. "What was fair about not telling me I had a baby on the way? What was fair about you going through a pregnancy all alone? What was fair about letting our little girl start her life without a daddy?"

"I did what I thought was best for all of us," she insisted.

"What *you* thought was best," he mocked. "You didn't even give me a chance to come up with a solution."

"Why should it have been your problem, your solution? I was the one who was pregnant."

"With my baby, dammit!" He closed his eyes, drew in a deep breath, then said more calmly, "We could have figured it out together."

"And done what? You'd be miserable away from White Pines. And I can't live there. It was as simple as that."

"We could have worked it out," he insisted with the stubborn conviction that was pure Adams. It didn't matter that they'd run into the same brick wall a thousand times before.

"And they're always telling me I'm the romantic," she said with a rueful sigh. "This time there wasn't a happy ending, Harlan Patrick. Trust me."

"Trust you," he hooted. "That's a laugh."

He regarded her evenly and took a step closer. He was near enough that she could feel the heat radiating from his body, smell the pure masculine scent of him. He reached out and ran his knuckle along the curve of her cheek, setting off goose bumps. She hated that he could make her react like that with just the skim of his fingers.

"Darlin', we've got a whole passel of passion, no question about that," he said. "We might even have a little love left. But I'm afraid trust is the one thing we'll never have between us again. You've pretty much seen to that, haven't you?"

Something died inside her at the cold, hard flatness of his words, but she knew it was the truth, had known it way back when she'd made the decision to keep the secret. Staying silent was going to cost her eventually. Now it had and it hurt more than she'd ever imagined.

"I'm sorry," she said again.

"*Sorry* won't cut it this time. Now how about getting this stuff together and taking me to see my daughter?"

It was a command, not a request, and it sent a jolt of pure fear shooting through her. "Tonight?"

"I think it's time, don't you? Way past time, in fact."

"She'll be asleep," she protested, trying to buy time. An hour from now she could bundle Amy Lynn up, wake the band and be on the bus heading for the next stop. No one would question the abrupt, middle-of-the-night departure, not aloud at any rate, and definitely not once they'd heard about Harlan Patrick's untimely arrival.

He gave her a look that suggested he saw straight through her. "I'll be quiet as a church mouse," he countered. "And if she happens to wake up, well, I'd say a momentous occasion like this is worth losing a little sleep over, wouldn't you?"

Laurie couldn't think of a single argument that could possibly counter the bitter logic of that. "Give me five minutes," she said tightly, then waited for him to leave the room.

He didn't budge. Regarding her evenly, he said with wry humor, "You surely weren't thinking I'd wait outside, were you? With that big old window right over your dressing table? I don't think so. As I recall, climbing out windows in the middle of the night used to be one of your specialties. That's how we got around your curfew way back when we couldn't keep our hands off each other."

"I was a kid back then," she protested, then gave up. He was sticking to her like glue, and that was that. "Okay, then, at least turn your back."

"Laurie, there's not an inch of bare skin on your body I haven't seen with my own eyes. It's a little late to turn all prim and proper on me."

She thought she detected a faint hint of laughter in his voice, and that alone was enough to give her hope that they could get through this mess tonight and go on with their lives. This was Harlan Patrick, after all. He'd always been quick to anger, but just as quick to forgive. He'd see Amy Lynn, satisfy himself that she was okay and go back to Texas. That would be that, she thought optimistically.

One glance at his expression told her she was delusional. Harlan Patrick wasn't going anywhere. And once he'd seen Amy Lynn, what then? Would he really be able to walk away, or would that just be the beginning of her worst nightmare? Mad as he was, she couldn't envision him demanding marriage at the moment. Would he try to take her baby? It was a distinct possibility.

Already gearing up for the fight, she scowled at him. "Oh, for heaven's sakes," she said, "if you're so hard up you have to sneak a peek at my bare breasts, then have yourself a ball."

She stripped out of her damp stage clothes and reached for fresh underwear. Only then did she notice that it wasn't strewed all over the room the way she'd left it.

Without bothering to cover herself, she turned to him, laughter bubbling up. "You straightened up in here, didn't you?"

He shot her a defiant look. "So what if I did?"

"Harlan Patrick Adams, I'm surprised at you. I thought you were long past tidying up my messes."

"Old habits die hard, darlin'," he said in a tone rich with hidden meanings. "Maybe you should remember that."

Chapter Four

Seeing Laurie again stirred up all the old feelings for Harlan Patrick. From love to hate, from bitterness to joy, his emotions went on a sixty-second roller-coaster ride, leaving his palms sweaty and his belly in knots. After that things only got worse.

Pure lust slammed through him the instant she walked in that dressing-room door. No woman had ever been her equal for making his temper hot and his body hotter. Having her stare him down with hardly a stitch of clothes on had just about broken his resolve to keep his hands to himself until they had this whole sorry situation straightened out. He was just itching to kiss her senseless, to lose himself in her warmth and her scent, to prove to himself that at least one thing hadn't changed between them.

There'd been a time when he'd have gone for it, taken the immediate satisfaction, reveled in the sensory explosion without a thought to the consequences. A few years of loneliness and loss had made him more cautious, maybe even more mature. In one tiny corner of his brain, it registered that sex wasn't the answer.

For once he jammed his hands in his pockets and stayed as far away from her as it was possible to get in that itty-bitty dressing room. It wasn't quite as far as good sense called for, but it was as far as he dared given the likelihood that she'd run out on him at the first opportunity. It had taken too long finding her for him to risk losing track of her again. He wasn't going anywhere until he'd seen his daughter and he and Laurie had made some decisions about the future.

Not that she was in much of a decision-making mood. In fact, he suspected she was going to be thoroughly unreasonable, just the way she'd always been when she'd been cornered. Normally he'd spend a lot of time trying to coax her into a better frame of mind, but there wasn't time for that, either. She and his baby girl were likely to slip right through his fingers before he could blink if he didn't stay right on top of Laurie every second, if he didn't make it perfectly clear what his own expectations were.

"I'm ready," she announced, drawing his attention.

She'd wiped away the last traces of stage makeup, leaving only a touch of lipstick. The glittery outfit

she'd worn had been replaced by worn jeans and a
T-shirt. She'd scooped her hair up into a careless
ponytail, just as she had as a girl when the heat of
a Texas summer afternoon got to be too much. His
fingers itched to pull away the band holding it, al-
lowing it to fall free again, the way he liked it.

Finally, though, he thought, she looked like his
Laurie, approachable and unassuming, the girl next
door. In some ways that was more dangerous than
the sexy woman who'd walked into the dressing
room a half hour before. He'd fallen in love with
the girl from his old hometown, not the superstar
image. He'd convinced himself that that Laurie,
wide-eyed with wonder, had gotten lost.

Of course, the change was superficial, all about
appearances. Try as he might, he couldn't tell yet
how deep the changes ran, if there was anything of
the old Laurie in her heart.

He stood up and took her small suitcase. It
weighed a ton. He grinned. "Still don't have a clue
how to pack light, do you? What's in here? Rocks?"

"If you're going to complain all the way back to
the hotel, I'll carry it," she said, reaching for it.
"I've been on my own a long time, Harlan Patrick.
I don't need you."

He grinned at the quick flare of temper. "You
must be out of sorts if you can't take a joke."

"I lost my sense of humor when I found you in
my dressing room."

He laughed at her disgruntled expression. "Careful, darlin', or you'll hurt my feelings."

"Not with your thick hide," she muttered under her breath as she sashayed past him.

"I heard that."

She ignored him and gave the guard a quick hug. "Thanks for everything, Chester."

The red-faced guard gave her a smile and Harlan Patrick a suspicious look, clearly wondering how he'd turned up in her dressing room. "Is everything okay, Laurie?"

"Everything's fine, Chester. This is an old…" She hesitated as if she couldn't quite decide how to describe Harlan Patrick. "Friend," she said finally. "Mr. Adams is an old friend from Texas."

The guard accepted the explanation readily enough and beamed at him. "Well, then, it's a pleasure to meet you, sir. I'll bet you're proud of our Miss Laurie."

"I am indeed," Harlan Patrick said.

After they'd left the building, Laurie glanced up at him. "You almost sounded as if you meant that."

"I did," he said simply, then sighed. "Even though your career came between us, I'm glad you made it because it's all that ever mattered to you. I'd hate to think you gave up all we had and had found nothing to replace it."

"It didn't replace it," she countered. "You mattered to me, Harlan Patrick. You still do."

"Just not enough," he said bitterly.

"Please, it wasn't like that. If there'd been another way…"

"You mean like me giving up White Pines."

"No," she retorted, then she was the one who

sighed. ''Yes, I suppose that was the only other alternative, at least at the beginning. Can you see now why I said it would have been impossible for us to find a solution when I got pregnant? We live in two different worlds, Harlan Patrick, literally.''

''Two different cities,'' he corrected as if the distinction made a difference, knowing it didn't.

''Whatever. You have to admit it was an impossible situation.''

''No. What I see is that our baby wasn't important enough for you to even try.''

Her hand connected with his cheek before he even realized what she intended. ''Don't you ever say something like that, Harlan Patrick Adams. Not ever. Our baby is the most important thing in my life.''

Harlan Patrick rubbed his cheek, but he didn't back down. ''What would happen if it came to a choice between her and your music, Laurie? What then? What happens when it's time for her to go to school? Will she lose then the same way I did? Will you shuffle her off to some boarding school?''

He let those words hang in the air as he opened the rental-car trunk and tossed her suitcase inside. He noticed that she was very subdued as she joined him. She got into the car without a word and, aside from giving him directions, she remained silent all the way to the hotel.

It was an old hotel, three stories high with a creaky elevator and a half-asleep clerk behind the desk. In the lobby Laurie paused. ''Please wait until morning to see the baby,'' she pleaded for the second time that night.

Harlan Patrick met her gaze evenly, then slowly shook his head. "I can't.''

"Because you don't trust me to be here in the morning.''

"That,'' he agreed, "and because I can't wait any longer. I want to see my daughter, Laurie. I want to hold her and discover whether she smells like talcum powder the way all the Adams babies do. I want to look into those blue eyes of hers and see if she instinctively recognizes her daddy. You owe me that.''

She gave in then without another argument and led the way to her suite on the second floor. He didn't doubt that it was luxurious by the hotel's standards, but the two rooms were probably half the size of what she was used to and furnished in an eclectic mix of styles that aimed for comfort, not fashion.

There was a young woman curled up on the chintz-covered couch with an open book in her lap. One look at Harlan Patrick and her mouth gaped. Her gaze snapped from him to Laurie and back again.

"Uh-oh,'' she murmured as she stood up. Her worried gaze landed on Laurie again. "Is there anything you'd like me to do?''

Harlan Patrick grinned at the unspoken willingness to call out the security troops if need be. Laurie shook her head.

"It's okay, Val. I can manage Mr. Adams.''

Val looked skeptical. "If you say so.'' She edged

toward the door with obvious reluctance. "If you need anything, anything at all…"

"I know where to find you," Laurie replied. "Thanks. Is the baby okay?"

"Sleeping like a little angel," Val assured her. "She had a bottle about an hour ago and drifted right off." She cast one last worried look at him, then shrugged. "I'll see you in the morning, then."

Laurie nodded. "Good night, Val."

When Val had gone, Harlan Patrick studied Laurie. "Are all of your employees willing to go the extra mile for you?"

"Pretty much." A smile hovered on her lips. "Some of the guys in the band can swing a mean guitar and they do love a brawl. You might want to remember that."

The echo of his earlier taunt hung in the air. Finally he nodded his agreement. "Duly warned."

Now that they were actually in her room, she seemed at a loss. Clearly she wasn't going to take him to his daughter without more prompting.

"Where is she?" he asked finally, then gestured toward what seemed likely to be the bedroom door. "In there?"

Laurie looked as if she'd like to deny it, but she finally shrugged. "Yes." She rested a hand against his sleeve. "Please, Harlan Patrick, don't wake her."

"I told you I wouldn't." He headed for the bedroom, then stopped when he realized she wasn't following. "Aren't you coming with me? Or don't you want to be around when a daddy sees his baby for the first time? Can't say I blame you. It could set off a whole streak of guilt.''

Tears welled up in her eyes at that, and he wondered if he'd pushed her too far with his sarcasm and anger. He wanted to hurt her, though, wanted her to know the kind of pain he'd been suffering from the moment he'd seen that baby's picture on the front page of that tabloid.

He turned away from her tears and strode into the bedroom, halting at the sight of a crib that had been set up in a corner. The puffy yellow gingham comforter with its design of daisies and ducks wasn't hotel issue. He was sure of that. Nor was the host of stuffed animals stuck around the sides like padding.

A huge lump formed in his throat as he crept closer. He felt the salty sting of tears as he caught his first glimpse of her with her diapered bottom poked in the air.

His first child, he thought, his throat choked with emotion. *His.*

By his calculations she was just over six months old now, a little plump and an Adams through and through. Bubbles formed at the corners of that little rosebud mouth, and her skin looked soft as satin. She was sleeping on her tummy with her still-damp thumb just a fraction of an inch from her mouth.

Words failed him. He just stood beside the crib and stared, stunned to discover that tears were welling up and overflowing. He was swamped by a feeling of protectiveness so deep, so powerful that it was all he could do not to grab her up and run with her back to White Pines where he could keep her safe always.

Instinctively he reached for her, then stopped himself as he remembered his promise not to wake her. But, oh, how he wanted to hold her, wanted to feel the weight of her in his arms, skim a knuckle over the delicate curve of her cheek. She was his precious first-born, and he didn't even know her name.

Realizing that brought back the anger, but he held it in check. Later there would be plenty of time for more recriminations. Right now he wanted only to drink in the sight of this tiny baby who was a part of him.

A part of him and Laurie, he reminded himself. This should have been something they shared from beginning to end. He should have been there to see her body swollen with his child. He should have been able to place his hand on her belly and feel that first miraculous stirring of life inside her. He should have been in the delivery room, holding her hand, coaching her through every stage of her labor, watching their baby enter the world.

That was the way he'd always planned it. He'd envisioned the two of them together till the day they died, surrounded by kids and, later, grandkids, maybe even great-grandkids, just the way Grandpa Harlan was, with White Pines as the center of their universe.

It wasn't supposed to be like this, with Laurie off on her own, pregnant, then having a baby in secret with no one by her side to share the joy. He wasn't supposed to be finding out he was a daddy from a blasted newspaper, then chasing all to hell and gone to find his child.

With his hands clenched into white-knuckled fists, he sensed Laurie beside him, but she hadn't said a word. As if she understood his turmoil, though, she reached out and tentatively covered his hand with her own. Almost despite himself, he relaxed at the touch, folded his fingers around hers.

"She's beautiful," he said finally, his voice choked with wonder.

"She is, isn't she?" she said with evident pride.

"What's her name, Laurie? I don't even know that much."

"Amy Lynn."

"Amy Lynn," he repeated in a whisper, his gaze on the baby. As the name sank in, he smiled. "Just like we planned." He faced Laurie. "You remembered that, didn't you? You remembered we talked about naming our first baby Amy Lynn if she was a girl. Amy because it was from your favorite book, *Little Women,* and we both liked it, and Lynn after my sister."

"And Cody if he was a boy, after your dad," she said.

Harlan Patrick closed his eyes against the fresh tide of memories that washed over him. So many dreams, so many innocent plans lost, and all because he and Laurie had never learned the meaning of compromise.

"Tell me everything," he pleaded. "From the minute you found out you were pregnant, I want to hear it all."

She shot him a rueful look. "Including all the gory morning-sickness details?"

"Everything," he said adamantly. "I figure I've got a lot to catch up on, better than a year."

Laurie regarded him with a resigned expression. "Then we'd better go into the other room and order up coffee. It's going to be a long night."

Harlan Patrick didn't care how long it took or how exhausted he was. Two pots of coffee made him jittery, but the details Laurie provided only made him want to know more. He listened and kept silent for hours on end, ignoring the sharp pangs of anger that rose up again and again as she described moments that could never be recaptured. Regrets piled up over what he'd missed through no fault of his own.

"Are there pictures?" he asked finally. "Of when you were pregnant? Of the baby when she was born?"

"Yes. Back in Nashville. There are several rolls of film from this trip that need to be developed. We just haven't been any place long enough to take it in."

He would have to be patient, but he would see them eventually, and then maybe some of this sense of loss, this feeling of having missed out on so much, would diminish. He wondered, though, if any scrapbook could ever take the place of real memories.

"Is she a good baby?"

"The best. She loves all the attention from the

band and she doesn't even mind all the traveling. In fact, riding on the bus seems to lull her to sleep."

"Are you sure the bus is well ventilated?" he fretted. "Maybe there's carbon monoxide leaking in, maybe that's why she sleeps so well."

Laurie shook her head at the leap his imagination had taken. "The bus is fine, Harlan Patrick. I'm not going to do anything to endanger the baby's life."

"Maybe you shouldn't even be on a bus. Maybe it would be better if you flew."

"The bus is equipped with every convenience imaginable," she protested. "Besides, I like traveling with Val and the whole band. I get some of my best songs written while we're on the road."

His temper flared again. "It's always about you, isn't it? What about what's best for the baby?"

Clearly undaunted by the accusation, she regarded him evenly. "That's not fair and you know it."

"No," he said, just as calmly, "I don't. I haven't been a part of your life for a very long time, but that's about to change."

There was a flicker of panic in her eyes then, but her voice was steady. "Meaning…?"

"What the hell do you think it means?" he asked heatedly. "It means that as of now I'm sticking to you like glue. Forget about running. Forget about hiding."

She winced. "I can see I was right about one thing."

"Which is?"

"I see where Amy Lynn got her temper. She's definitely her daddy's girl. She already has the family stubborn streak. Most babies don't learn to say no until they're two. Amy Lynn may not be able to say it yet, but she sure can make her preferences known.'' She gave him a pointed look. ''I'm not sure it's a legacy you ought to be proud of.''

Maybe he deserved the censure. He was stubborn. He was an Adams. It came with the genes and from his perspective, it wasn't a bad trait to inherit. Call it stubbornness or persistence—to his way of thinking it was the same as commitment and staying power. He wasn't about to let Laurie's accusation throw him off course.

Facing her, he said fiercely, ''I want my daughter to be a part of my life, Laurie. I want her to know she's an Adams. I'll fight you for that if I have to.''

He saw the tumble of fear, followed by resignation in her expression. Clearly she'd been anticipating something like this ever since he'd turned up.

''I won't fight you,'' she said quietly. ''We'll work something out. When she's a little older, she can come to the ranch as often as you'd like.''

And have his daughter think of him as a distant stranger? There was no chance in hell he'd buy a plan like that. He scowled at Laurie.

''I mean starting now,'' he said, his tone implacable.

''But she's just a baby,'' Laurie protested.

''And I'm every bit as capable of caring for her as you are. More capable, in fact. At least I have a home I stay in, instead of moving from hotel to hotel. She wouldn't be turned over to nannies. She'd be surrounded by family, including your own mother, I might add.'' He regarded her pointedly. ''Best of all, she wouldn't be getting her picture plastered all over the front of the tabloids.''

Laurie flinched at that, but came back fighting. ''That picture was what brought her to your attention,'' she reminded him. ''Maybe you ought to send a thank-you note to the photographer.''

''You mean you haven't already had him strung up for giving away your little secret?''

''Believe me, if I'd had any recourse at all, I would have taken it,'' she said fervently. ''No one wanted you to find out about Amy Lynn this way, least of all me.''

''No,'' he agreed quietly. ''You never wanted me to find out about her at all.''

He noticed she didn't try to deny it. Instead, she rubbed her eyes in a gesture that was as familiar to him as the feel of her skin. Laurie'd always stayed awake past exhaustion because she never wanted to miss a thing. If he'd been in a kinder frame of mind, he'd have seen it earlier and insisted that they both get the sleep they sorely needed. He did suggest it now.

''Go to bed, Laurie. We'll finish this conversation in the morning.''

He caught the quick flash of relief in her eyes and guessed exactly what was on her mind. ''You aren't thinking of skipping out during the night, are you, darlin'?''

Color tinted her cheeks pink. ''Of course not,'' she denied a little too hastily. ''I'll be right here when you get back in the morning. I promise.''

He smiled at the solemn vow. He figured it wasn't worth spit. "Of course you will be," he said agreeably. "And I'm sure you won't mind if I just take a precaution or two."

"Such as?"

"Well, for starters, I'll be sleeping right in there next to you."

She swallowed hard at that. Color flamed in her cheeks. "I don't think so."

"You don't have any choice in the matter."

"It's a bad idea," she insisted.

"Why? Afraid you won't be able to resist me?"

"*That* is not the issue."

"Then what is?"

"It's just wrong, that's all."

"You'll have to do better than that, darlin'. You've had my baby. It's a little late to get all prissy about sharing a bed with me."

She opened her mouth, then snapped it shut again. As regally as any queen, she rose from the sofa and headed for the bedroom. She was almost at the door when Harlan Patrick realized that if he didn't hightail it across the room, she'd have that door slammed and locked before he could blink. As it was, he barely got his foot wedged into the crack when she tried to close the door in his face.

"Nice try," he enthused as he waltzed into the bedroom behind her.

Her shoulders slumped. "Oh, have it your way. If you'll feel better forcing your way into my bed, then so be it."

Her phrasing rankled, but Harlan Patrick didn't

back down as she'd obviously hoped he would. He tugged off his boots, then stretched out on top of the covers.

"See, darlin', my intentions are honorable. I'm not even shucking my jeans."

"What a saint."

He leveled a smoldering look at her then. "Not a saint, Laurie. You'd be wise to remember that before you start testing me."

"I have no intention of testing you," she insisted, giving him a haughty look before going into the bathroom and closing the door emphatically behind her.

When she came out again, she was wearing a too-big Dallas Cowboys T-shirt that reached to midthigh and brought a smile to his lips. If he wasn't very much mistaken, it was the very same shirt he had given her on her last visit to Texas, a shirt he'd worn until it was faded and one she'd loved because it carried the scent of him. He wondered if she remembered that when she'd put it on or if she'd simply hoped that he'd forgotten.

She turned out the light on her way to the bed, then slid beneath the covers. The mattress wasn't what it could have been. It sagged under his weight, which eventually caused her to roll toward him despite her best efforts to cling to her own side.

Harlan Patrick was still wide awake when she settled against him. He heard her soft exhale of breath and felt her snuggle just a little tighter. That was the second time in twenty-four hours when it took every ounce of willpower he possessed to keep his promise and keep his hands off of the woman he loved.

Chapter Five

A baby's soft whimpers jarred Harlan Patrick out of a restless sleep that had lasted all of a half hour. For a minute he had no idea where he was or why a baby might be nearby. Then he felt the once familiar whisper of Laurie's breath fanning across his cheek, felt the weight of her arm resting on his chest, sniffed the rose-petal scent of her perfume.

It all came flooding back to him then, the tabloid, the trip to Nashville, the rush to Montana. Those whimpering cries, which he judged from experience with what seemed like a zillion nieces and nephews and second cousins, were about to turn into a full-throated yowling.

Miracle of miracles, he recognized that those cries were coming from his daughter. *His daughter.* What an unexpected blessing.

He eased out of the bed and padded over to the crib. At his arrival the baby seemed to take a deep breath and wait, as if trying to decide whether the whimpers had accomplished her goal or if more-strenuous cries were necessary. Blue eyes, shimmering with tears, stared solemnly back at him. He felt his heart turn over in his chest.

"Don't cry, precious girl. Daddy's here," he whispered as he picked her up and cradled her in his arms.

"Daddy's here," he said again a little more emphatically as he carried her into the living room of the suite and settled into a chair with her, awestruck with the wonder of holding his own child in his arms.

The whimpers subsided the instant he picked her up, but he figured it wouldn't be long before they started up again unless he figured out what had brought them on in the first place. Again years of experience with other people's kids kicked in.

"So, what's the deal?" he asked. "You wet? Hungry? Maybe both?"

She seemed to study him quizzically, either trying to make sense of his words or trying to weigh whether or not to trust him. Suddenly that little rosebud mouth tilted into a crooked smile that came pretty darned close to breaking his heart.

"Did I guess right?" he asked conversationally. "I'll bet there's a diaper bag around here somewhere, but what about a bottle? Any ideas?"

She gurgled at him happily, as if imparting the

information he'd requested. Unfortunately he didn't have a clue how to interpret it.

Tucking her against his shoulder, he searched for supplies. As he'd anticipated, the diaper was easy enough to come by and no challenge at all to put on. The bottle had him stymied. He wondered if room service was up to the challenge, or was this something for the invaluable Val, whose last name and room number he didn't know?

When he was about to concede that he was going to have to wake Laurie, he was struck by an inspiration. There was a tiny refrigerator in the room. Under normal circumstances it would be stocked with sodas and liquor and overpriced snacks, but maybe Laurie Jensen would rate a selection of baby bottles instead. He used the key that had been left lying on top of the refrigerator. Sure enough, there was a handful of bottles tucked inside.

"See there, darlin', Daddy's not going to let you down. We just have one little problem left. Something tells me you won't like this stuff if it's cold as ice."

He glanced around, but there was no sign of a microwave. He could think of only one alternative. "Shall we take a little stroll down to the hotel kitchen and have it heated? I know it's barely daybreak, but surely someone will be stirring down there."

Amy Lynn gurgled in apparent agreement.

He propped the baby against a nest of pillows while he paused to tug on his boots. Even the momentary abandonment almost brought on a fresh bout of tears. The instant he had her back in his arms, she beamed at him approvingly, clearly pleased that he was catching on. He slipped quietly out of the room and carried her and the bottle downstairs.

The only waitress on duty in the hotel restaurant at that early hour took one look at the two of them and rushed to help.

Harlan Patrick held out the bottle. "Help? I know you're probably not quite ready to open, but we have a little emergency here."

"No problem. I'll have that heated right up for you," she said, taking the bottle and giving him a less than surreptitious once-over. "Just have a seat at that table over there by the window. It's got the best view in the room. The sun ought to be sneaking up over the mountains any minute now. You want a cup of coffee when I come back, sugar? It should be just about ready by now."

Harlan Patrick thought of the acid already churning in his stomach from last night's caffeine overdose and shook his head. "Maybe a big glass of orange juice and some toast, if it's not too much trouble."

"Coming right up," she promised.

She was back in no time with the juice, the toast and the heated bottle. His daughter took the bottle and began sucking lustily. He grinned at her enthusiasm. "Most definitely an Adams," he observed. "We all have healthy appetites."

"She's a beautiful baby," the waitress said.

"Isn't she?"

"And you're a natural with her. She's a lucky kid."

Harlan Patrick grinned. "Thanks."

"You give a holler if you need anything else."

He glanced at his daughter. "Oh, I think we're all set now."

After the waitress had gone, he held Amy Lynn contentedly while she finished the bottle, staring at her in awe, still unable to believe he'd had a part in creating anything this perfect, this fragile. This time alone with her reassured him that his determination to make a place for himself in her life was well-founded. He'd always wanted kids, but it had been an abstract kind of longing, something he pictured in his future with Laurie. Amy Lynn was real, and the protective paternal sensations she stirred in him were overwhelming.

Just when he was finishing up his juice and thinking it was time to go back upstairs, all hell broke loose. Security guards, trailed by a frantic Laurie, still wearing only the Dallas Cowboys T-shirt, along with Val and several men Harlan Patrick guessed were members of the band came charging into the dining room.

"There," Laurie shouted, pointing at him and practically quivering with outrage. "There he is. He's trying to steal my baby."

Harlan Patrick reacted with stunned silence to the outrageous accusation.

Even before the guards could react, Laurie rushed across the room and tried to snatch Amy Lynn from

Harlan Patrick's arms. He stared at her and held the baby out of reach.

"Have you lost your mind?" he asked Laurie in a deceptively mild tone as men surrounded him.

"You took her," she accused. "You took her without my permission."

When one of the guards reached for him, Harlan Patrick shot a quelling look in his direction that instantly had the man backing off.

"Ms. Jensen, it looks like your baby's just fine," one guard suggested quietly. "He hasn't gone anywhere with her."

"He just brought her down for a bottle," the waitress chimed in. "What in heaven's name is all the fuss about?"

"He took her from my room," Laurie whispered, sinking onto a chair beside him as the fight drained out of her. "I woke up, and my baby was gone."

Harlan Patrick finally understood her hysteria. In a fleeting, half-awake daze, she had thought he'd taken off with the baby. It was ironic given his own fears that she'd do the very same thing if given a chance. Still, he cursed himself for not thinking to leave a note. He'd never meant to scare her to death. He'd just assumed she wouldn't awaken before he returned.

"Darlin', you knew she was with me," he reminded her quietly. "You had to know no harm would come to her."

"Don't you see?" she replied in a choked voice. "That's why I was so terrified."

"You thought I'd run off with her," he said, voicing his earlier assessment of her overreaction.

She nodded, and this time when she reached for Amy Lynn, he placed the baby in her arms. Then he tucked a finger under Laurie's chin and forced her to face him. Her eyes shimmered with unshed tears, and her chin wobbled.

"Listen to me," he commanded gently. "No matter what happens between us, no matter how angry I get or how frustrated, I will never just walk away with Amy Lynn. You have my solemn vow on that. Whatever happens, the two of us will decide it together, okay?"

Her gaze locked with his. "You swear it?"

"On my honor."

A sigh shuddered through her then. One glance at Val was all it took for the security guards and the band members to melt away, leaving the three of them alone—Harlan Patrick, Laurie and the baby. Even the friendly waitress seemed to know enough to steer clear.

"You okay?" Harlan Patrick asked eventually.

Laurie gave him a halfhearted smile. "Just embarrassed over the fuss I caused."

He grinned. "If you're feeling that way now, then there's no telling how you're going to react when you realize you're in the middle of a public restaurant wearing nothing but a big ol' T-shirt."

She glanced down at herself and moaned. Then she scowled at him. "This is your fault, you know."

He nodded solemnly. "I know. And I am sorry. The baby was hungry and I wanted to get her fed without waking you. I thought I was being clever to think of coming down here to get her bottle warmed.''

''A noble intention,'' she agreed, ''but then yours usually are. That's never meant you couldn't find some way to turn my life upside down in the process.''

He nodded at that, too. ''It's been my pleasure,'' he said with a grin. ''Yours, too, if I remember correctly.''

''Sometimes,'' she conceded. ''But we're supposed to be responsible adults now. We have a child, for goodness' sakes.''

It was exactly the opening he'd been waiting for. ''I'm glad you can see that. I have a suggestion.''

''What's that?''

''Let's prove just how responsible we are. Let's get married.''

The suggestion was made impulsively. Harlan Patrick had no idea when he'd reached any decision that marriage was the route they should take. If he was startled by the words coming out of his mouth, though, Laurie looked as if he'd suggested they go snowboarding stark naked.

''Oh, no, you don't,'' she said, hitching her chair backward to get away from him as if his very nearness was somehow threatening.

''Don't what?''

''You are not going to manipulate me into marrying you, Harlan Patrick Adams,'' she said with fire in her eyes.

"I wasn't aware I was manipulating. I thought I was proposing."

"In this case, it's the same difference."

"And you say the stubborn genes are all on the Adams side," he taunted. "Laurie, let's be logical for a minute. Amy Lynn is mine. I want her to have my name."

"She already does," she confessed in a whisper.

This time he stared. "What?"

"I put your name on the birth certificate. I never wanted there to be any doubt about that, at least. So, you see, marrying me would be superfluous."

He grinned at the airy declaration. "Is that what you call being my wife? I could take offense."

"You know what I meant," she retorted with a defiant jut of her chin.

He debated arguing with her, then decided to leave well enough alone. He might have lost the battle, but the war could be won another day.

"Okay," he conceded. "I can see I'm not going to get anywhere this morning. Just think about it. We have plenty of time to decide. I'm not going anywhere." He shot her a wicked look. "You, however, might want to find out if there's a back way out of here. Otherwise the next tabloid picture you're in is likely to be a whole lot more revealing than either of us would like."

Laurie's nerves didn't settle down until after she was back in the suite and had spent an hour with Amy Lynn tucked securely in her arms. Those few minutes before she'd found the baby downstairs with Harlan Patrick had been the most terrifying of her life. Even though she knew him as well as she knew herself, she had wondered for just an instant if he was so furious with her that he'd be capable of kidnapping their baby.

Not that it would have been all that hard to trace him, she admitted. There wasn't a doubt in her mind that he would make a beeline for White Pines to show his daughter off to his family.

His proposal on the heels of that upset had been enough to thoroughly shake her. It was difficult enough to cope with Harlan Patrick when he was angry and unreasonable. It was even more difficult to fend him off when he was being quietly reasonable and persistent.

Of course, this was hardly the first time the question of marriage had come up between them. She smiled as she recalled the first time he'd asked, way back in high school on the night of his senior prom. They'd been in the back seat of a convertible, staring up at the stars. She'd turned him down then and every time since.

Even in high school, when she had been starry-eyed and madly in love with him, she had known instinctively that she would never be content as his wife unless she had really tried to make a career out of her music. He had never understood how much it meant to her, nor why she couldn't be happy just singing in a local club every now and then or maybe just with the church choir. He simply hadn't comprehended her ambition and her desperate hunger for success.

Sometimes she hadn't fully understood the need herself, though she suspected it had a lot to do with the hand-to-mouth existence she and her mother had led. She'd wanted to be independent enough to survive on her own without relying on the whims of a man—even Harlan Patrick—to provide for her needs.

Harlan Patrick had everything in the world he wanted right there in Los Piños, Texas. His ranch. His family. She wanted the world and the reassurance of having her own bank account, piled high with money she'd earned herself, money she knew she could replace herself if the need arose.

She glanced across the room to find his gaze on her. He was sprawled in a chair, his expression speculative, as if he were trying to puzzle out which buttons to push to get her to come around to his point of view. It was disconcerting, because she knew that sooner or later he would figure it out. He always had. The only time she'd ever said no to him and stuck to it was on the subject of marriage. With Amy Lynn to consider and more money in the bank than she could ever spend, she wasn't sure how long it would be before she gave in on that, as well.

"You still mad at me?" he asked finally.

"No."

"I really didn't mean to frighten you."

"I know that."

"So, what's on the agenda for today?"

Laurie glanced at her watch. "We need to pack up and be on the bus in an hour. The club I'm playing tonight is a couple of hours from here. That'll give us time to get there, set up, test the sound system and rehearse for an hour or so.'' Even though she suspected she already knew the answer, she asked, ''What about you?''

''Where you go, I go.''

She sighed. ''For how long, Harlan Patrick?''

He gave her an all too familiar stubborn look. ''As long as it takes.''

''What about the ranch?''

''Daddy's there and Grandpa Harlan. They can get by without me for a while.''

She hesitated, then said, ''I spoke with your grandfather the other day.''

His eyes widened with surprise. ''How did that happen?''

''I called to see if you knew about the tabloid,'' she admitted ruefully. ''Based on what he said about you taking off for parts unknown, I gathered you did, but he didn't.''

''He probably does by now. He probably started asking questions the instant he hung up. Mama and Sharon Lynn no doubt gave him an earful.''

''They know, then?''

''Oh yeah, they know. Sharon Lynn was the one who brought the paper out to the ranch. They were scheming to buy up every copy in town and burn them, when I walked in.''

''Your sister used to tolerate me well enough because she knew you cared about me, but she must really hate me now,'' Laurie said with unmistakable regret. For so many years all she had wanted was to fit in, to be accepted by this wonderful, loving family.

"Let's just say I'd be careful about ordering any food from her next time you stop by Dolan's," Harlan Patrick told her with a crooked grin exactly like the baby's. "Big sisters have a way of carrying loyalty to extremes."

"I wouldn't know," she said, unable to hide the trace of envy in her voice. "No sisters, no brothers. That's why I always loved going to the ranch with you. Even though it was just you and Sharon Lynn in your family, the extended Adams family was so huge and rambunctious."

"That's Grandpa Harlan's doing. He's not happy unless the place is crawling with family. He likes to think of himself as head of a ranching dynasty."

"He was very kind to me when I called. I doubt he will be the next time I show my face in Los Piños."

"Oh, darlin', you've got to be kidding. You're the mama of yet another great-grandbaby. You'll be welcomed with open arms. In fact, don't be surprised if he doesn't greet you, then introduce you to a minister and hand me a couple of gold bands."

"Now, there's a reason to stay away," she murmured.

Harlan Patrick chuckled. "I never took you for a coward. You don't have a bit of trouble saying no to me. Are you saying you won't be able to resist granddaddy's matchmaking?"

"You know I've always respected your grandfather."

"And?"

"And yes, it would be hard to ignore his wishes. I would hate to have him think less of me."

"Guess that tells me where I rank in the Adams hierarchy."

"Don't pout, Harlan Patrick. When you're eighty, I'll probably listen to you, too."

"In the meantime you've just given me a tremendous incentive to lure you back to Texas."

She regarded him with a stubborn lift to her chin. "I am not going anywhere near Texas, so you can just forget about that."

He shrugged. "Then I'll just have to figure out how to be more persuasive in Montana, Texas, Tennessee or wherever else you intend to run to hide out."

"I'm not hiding out. I'm working."

"From where I sit, it looks like the same difference."

Laurie couldn't take any more. The worst part about Harlan Patrick's accusation was that it was true. The further she ran, the busier she stayed, the less she had to think about Amy Lynn's daddy and the sneaky way he had of stirring up vivid memories and wicked sensations.

The instant she stood up, though, the baby began to cry. Harlan Patrick was on his feet in a heartbeat, reaching for Amy Lynn and murmuring soothingly until she quieted at once in his arms. Laurie scowled at the two of them—one a persistent, clever devil, the other a tiny traitor.

"I'm going to go in and pack," she said, and

whirled around to leave the room. If she spent too much time witnessing the wonderful, instantaneous bonding between Amy Lynn and her daddy, she would never in a million years be able to keep Harlan Patrick on the fringes of their lives.

At the doorway to the bedroom, she glanced back to find Harlan Patrick totally absorbed with his daughter. He was regarding her as if she were the most magnificent, mysterious creature on earth. Which, of course, she was, Laurie conceded with motherly pride.

Watching the two of them, she realized that in less than twenty-four hours the plan she'd had to keep Harlan Patrick at bay had totally and thoroughly unraveled. She would never keep him on the fringes of their lives as she had hoped just moments ago. He was already smack-dab in the middle of their world. And one thing she knew about Harlan Patrick—about any Adams—was that budging him once he'd gotten so much as a toehold was all but impossible.

For better or worse, Harlan Patrick was in their lives to stay.

Chapter Six

Once he'd lost the first round in his fight to claim Laurie as his wife, Harlan Patrick didn't even have to think twice about what he was going to do. For as long as it took to win them over, he intended to stick to Laurie and Amy Lynn like glue.

First he called Jordan and made arrangements to have his uncle's plane picked up in Montana and flown back to Texas. Next he called his father and arranged for an extended vacation from the ranch. He'd expected an argument and was surprised when he didn't get one. He was even more surprised when his father began to probe more deeply into his reasons for staying away.

"Do you still love her?" Cody Adams asked him point-blank, proving that the family grapevine was in fine working order and engaging in a whole lot of speculation.

He hesitated, then admitted, "Right now a part of me is still furious with her, but yes, I love her. I always have."

"And you're happy about being a daddy?"

There wasn't even a split second of hesitation before he responded to that one. "It's amazing, Dad. I've never felt anything like it. Just wait till you see Amy Lynn," he said. "She's a little angel. How could I be anything but happy about her? She'll steal your heart, too."

"Then take my advice, son. Don't take no for an answer. They're your family. You fight for them any way you have to."

"Even if I have to play down and dirty?" he inquired lightly, thinking of how he could always bend Laurie to his will with a couple of well-timed kisses.

"Whatever works," his father agreed. "I pulled out all the stops with your mama and I've never regretted it. The situations are not all that dissimilar, you know. She'd had your sister without telling me, and I came back to Texas to discover I had a ready-made family. I was furious, but once I got beyond casting blame I did everything except stand on my head and whistle the wedding march to get through to her. I'd have tried that, too, if I'd thought it would work."

"What did work finally?" he asked his father, not too proud to seek advice that might make a difference in his campaign to win Laurie.

His father laughed at his eagerness for surefire

answers. "You'd have to ask your mother that, but if I had to guess, I'd say it was the fact that I never gave up, that I stuck around even when she was being the most contrary female in all of Texas. She finally had to take me seriously." He chuckled. "Of course, she did wait till they were wheeling her into the delivery room to give birth to you before she finally gave in. I suppose she figured with two babies of mine, she didn't have a chance in hell of ever shaking me."

Harlan Patrick had heard the tale a thousand times before, but this time he was hearing it in a whole new light. This time it wasn't just a humorous family legend. It was inspiration for his own battle to win Laurie's heart and claim his family. If persistence was what it took, then he was already on the right track.

"Thanks for reminding me of that," he told his father.

"You just bring those two back home with you. They're what's important in your life right now. Family matters more than anything else, son, this ranch included. Your granddaddy would be the first to tell you that, and you know how he feels about this place. In the meantime he and I can manage the ranch. There are plenty of others in the family who'll pitch in if we need them to."

"Just don't forget that I'm the one who's going to get the place one day. I don't want you running it into the ground while I'm not looking."

"Very funny," his father said dryly. "Besides, with your granddaddy around, I don't think there's much chance of that. As old as I am, he'd still tan my hide if he thought I was messing with his legacy to all of you. Take care, son, and good luck with Laurie. If she's the woman you want, then I wish you only the best in getting her."

Harlan Patrick knew what it had cost his father to wish him luck. He'd been blaming Laurie for a long time now for mistreating his only son. Forgiving her would take some time, but Harlan Patrick didn't doubt that in the end his father truly did wish them well.

"Thanks," he said. "Something tells me I'm going to need all the luck I can get."

As he hung up, he realized that Laurie was standing in the doorway.

"Your father?"

"Yep."

"How is he?"

"Fine. He sends his regards."

She looked skeptical. "Is that so?"

"He told me to hurry up and come home with you and Amy Lynn."

She frowned. "Now, Harlan Patrick—"

He cut her off. "I know. You haven't agreed to go anywhere with me. I guess that leaves me with just one alternative."

"Which is?"

"I'll go with you."

Laurie looked shaken by the announcement, even though she had to know that it was what he'd intended all along. "With me?"

Harlan Patrick grinned. "That's right, darlin',

when that big ol' bus of yours pulls out of here, I'll be sitting in there right alongside you.''

"But the ranch..." she began hopefully.

"Covered."

"Didn't you say you flew here in Jordan's plane?" she asked with a note of desperation in her voice.

"I did. He's sending someone to get it."

Her expression fell. "I thought maybe you'd just fly to the next stop or rent a car or something."

"Not a chance."

"You'll hate being all cramped up on the bus."

"You like it, don't you?"

"Yes, but—"

"I'll manage, Laurie. If it's good enough for you and Amy Lynn, then it's good enough for me."

She stared at him silently, then asked, "You're going to pester me until you get your way, aren't you?"

He chuckled. "You've got that right. I gotta say I'm looking forward to it, too. Always did love a challenge."

"Does it matter at all to you that I am not looking forward to it?"

He regarded her solemnly. "Well, of course, it troubles me that you'd like to be rid of me, but if you're asking if that means I'll give up, the answer is no."

She sighed heavily. "I was afraid of that."

They sat across from each other in silence. Harlan Patrick knew from her irritated expression that Laurie was wrestling with herself, trying to decide whether she could get away with banishing him from her bus. He was confident she'd reach the right decision, so he didn't waste his energy trying to start a debate with her.

When the quiet had dragged on too long, he grinned. "Give it up, Laurie. You can't think of any way to get rid of me short of having a security guard hold me down while the bus drives off."

For an instant her expression brightened.

"Don't even think about it," he warned. "I'll just keep turning up like a bad penny, and my mood won't improve if you make it difficult for me."

"Why? Doesn't it matter that I don't want you around?"

The remark stung, though it shouldn't have, especially since he knew for a fact it wasn't true. She didn't really want him to go away. She was just scared that having him around would weaken her resolve, that she'd give in and marry him. She was probably right to be terrified of that, because making her his wife was exactly what he had every intention of accomplishing.

Reacting without thinking, he crossed the room and pulled her up and into his arms. His mouth found hers just as it opened to form a protest. The kiss went from an intended brush of his lips across hers to a deep, soul-searing possession in seconds. She tasted of minty toothpaste and surrounded him with some sweet, fresh scent from her morning shower, unadorned by the rose-petal perfume she favored. This was Laurie at her most basic—innocently alluring, unconsciously seductive.

His pulse pounded as tongues met and danced an old, familiar duel. His skin was on fire where her hands finally settled after an instant of protesting reluctance. His body throbbed with need as her hips cradled his arousal. He threaded his fingers through her hair, tangling in the long strands of silk. He withdrew from the kiss, gazed into her dazed eyes and went back for more.

But that brief hesitation had been enough to break the spell, long enough for her doubts to come flooding back, apparently, because she gave him a shove that took him by surprise and had him staggering back a step before he recovered.

There was fire sparkling in her eyes and a don't-you-dare expression on her lips when he grinned at her. "That's okay, darlin'. I think I proved my point."

She scowled. "And what point would that be?"

"That you're not immune to me, even after all this time. You just wish you were."

"Oh, go to blazes, Harlan Patrick," she all but shouted just as someone knocked on the door of the suite. Laurie raced to open it.

Harlan Patrick spotted Val on the doorstep and concluded that the kissing and the argument were at an end for now. Laurie wouldn't pursue either with an audience.

"You all set?" Val asked Laurie, though her speculative gaze was fixed squarely on Harlan Patrick.

Laurie nodded. "I'll get the bags."

"Want me to get Amy Lynn?" Val asked.

Harlan Patrick interceded. "I'll be bringing her," he announced, seizing the carrier in which the baby had been napping, along with his own bag.

Val's gaze shot from him to Laurie and back again. "You're coming, too?"

"I am," he confirmed.

She looked to her boss. "He is?"

Laurie shrugged. "Apparently so."

Val edged closer to her boss and lowered her voice. "How do you feel about that?"

"She's mad as a wet hen," Harlan Patrick supplied cheerfully.

"I asked her," Val noted.

Laurie glowered. "He has it right."

"I could make him disappear," Val offered. "All it would take would be a word to security."

"Don't waste your time," Laurie said with regret. "You might slow him down, but you won't get rid of him."

"But it's your bus, your tour," Val argued. "He has no right—"

"Now, that's where you're wrong," Harlan Patrick corrected mildly. He hoisted the baby carrier to draw attention to it. "This little girl gives me all sorts of rights."

To his satisfaction that seemed to be enough to silence both women. He doubted, though, that he'd heard the end of it, especially from Laurie.

On the bus Laurie headed straight for the back, hauling Val right along behind her and all but shoving her into one of the two custom-made lounge chairs that had replaced the half-dozen regular seats in the back to create a comfortable lounge. There was a table between the two seats with cup-holders built in. A small refrigerator had been tucked in on one side with a microwave atop it for heating Amy Lynn's bottles or the coffee the band consumed by the gallon. There was a built-in crib, as well, a recent addition that had been installed right after she gave birth. Laurie's guitar cases rested in a pile behind the seats.

Satisfied that Harlan Patrick was several rows in front of them with the baby's carrier seat-belted in beside him, Laurie sank down.

"Do you want something to drink?" Val asked, regarding her worriedly.

"Bottled water," Laurie said. "And a couple of aspirin."

"I imagine fending him off would be enough to give you a whopper of a headache," Val agreed, handing her the requested items. "He's a persistent guy, isn't he?"

"You don't know the half of it," Laurie muttered.

"Sexy, too."

"Are you planning to enumerate all of his attributes?" Laurie inquired testily.

Val grinned. "Nope, I think I'll just linger awhile on sexy. I haven't seen a man that gorgeous up close in a long, long time. You must have astounding willpower to have turned your back on him."

Laurie waved her off. "If you find him so blasted fascinating, you can go on up there and sit with him," she suggested. "Look to your heart's content. Keep him distracted."

"You wouldn't mind?" Val asked, sounding just a tad too eager.

"No. I've had a song buzzing around in my head for the past couple of hours. Maybe I can get some of it down."

"Something to do with cowboys and Texas, I'll bet," Val commented with a wink.

"No," Laurie denied. "Something about murder and mayhem on a country singer's tour bus."

That was enough to encourage Val to scoot out of the line of fire. She settled into a seat across the aisle from Harlan Patrick and attempted to engage him in conversation. Even though Val's move had been her idea, Laurie found she couldn't concentrate knowing that the two of them were chatting. When she heard Harlan Patrick's low, seductive laugh, her stomach knotted. When he leaned halfway across the aisle to whisper something to Val, it took all her willpower to stay in her own seat.

She was jealous, she realized with astonishment. In all the years she'd been in love with Harlan Patrick, he'd never given her cause to be jealous. Though plenty of girls in high school had chased after him, though he'd been a natural flirt, she'd never felt so much as a twinge of jealousy because she had always known that he was hers.

He claimed the same thing was true now, but just how long would he remain loyal with her pushing him away and declaring that she didn't want him back? Did it even matter, when nothing had changed? She lived half her life on the road. He was the ultimate homebody.

But he was here now, a nagging little voice reminded her. He had walked away from White Pines in the blink of an eye when he'd discovered he had a daughter. Could he walk away for good? She doubted it. This was temporary. He was just staking his claim, trying to get her to marry him and go back to Texas with him. He'd said nothing at all about making a long-term change in his life-style. The impasse was as overwhelming as ever.

Gary Whitakker, her lead guitarist and one of the kindest, gentlest guys she'd ever known, edged down the aisle and dropped into the seat Val had vacated. There'd been a time when she'd considered the possibility of a romance with him, but memories of Harlan Patrick had intruded every time the man had tried to kiss her. Eventually they'd settled for being friends.

"You doing okay?" he asked, searching her face for signs of distress.

"I've had better days," she admitted.

Gary glanced toward the row of seats in front of them. "He seems like a nice guy."

"He is."

"I saw the way he was looking at Amy Lynn when we found them in the hotel dining room. He already adores that baby girl. He's not going to walk away without a fight."

"I know."

"He looks at you the same way."

She gave him a rueful look. "I know that, too."

"He's the reason nothing ever happened between us, isn't he?"

She nodded.

"If you're so crazy about him, I'm not sure I see the problem."

"He's in Texas. I'm not."

To her irritation, he grinned. "Did you run out of cash for plane tickets?"

Laurie scowled. "You know, Gary, these pithy little observations of yours are getting on my nerves. Do you have any solutions?"

He had the audacity to chuckle at her display of temper. "In the words of a country-music superstar I know, you might try listening to your heart."

Good advice, Laurie conceded, but she couldn't risk taking it. Her heart's message was clear as a bell, but there were far-reaching implications that she simply couldn't deal with.

"Grab your guitar," she instructed instead, reaching for her own. "I've got a new song I want to play around with."

Like all of her musicians, Gary's eyes lit up at once at the prospect of creating another megahit. He listened as she strummed a few chords and picked up on her rhythm with the instinct of someone who'd grown accustomed to her creative process.

Laurie jotted down a few words, hummed a few bars, then tried the words aloud. It didn't take long before a few of the others were joining in and the bus was filled with the country-pop crossover sound that had taken her to the top of the charts.

She felt Harlan Patrick's eyes on her as her voice

rang out and wondered if he guessed that he was behind the heartbreak in the lyrics. She lifted her gaze and met his. All at once she was lost in those deep blue eyes, eyes that reflected understanding and love, so much love that it was all she could do not to weep.

Why was it, she wondered as she strummed the last chord and then fell silent, that sometimes love simply wasn't enough? Leaving Harlan Patrick not once but twice had hurt. She had anguished over it both times.

But having him back in her life again, having him so near and knowing that another parting was inevitable, was tearing her apart.

She heard Amy Lynn whimper and was half out of her seat in the blink of an eye. Harlan Patrick's gaze remained steady on hers for another instant, and then he broke eye contact and reached for the baby—their daughter, she reminded herself as tears stung her eyes, as much his as hers, though she'd tried to deny that for months now.

Sinking back into her seat, she watched father and child, unable to tear her gaze away from the adoration in Harlan Patrick's eyes. Already Amy Lynn seemed to recognize her daddy. She accepted his comfort, settled down at once in his arms. They were bonding, and she knew without a doubt that the ties forming now would be impossible to break.

"Mind a word of advice from a friend?" Gary inquired lightly, drawing her attention away from the scene being played out up the aisle.

"What?"

"Find a way to make it work."

"It's impossible," she said, unable to hide the despairing note in her voice.

"Nothing's impossible if you both want it badly enough."

She seared him with a look. "Let me ask you this. Would you give up everything we've accomplished the past few years and go back to singing backup in advertising jingles just to be with the woman you love?"

"You seem to forget, I've been divorced three times. I'm not sure I've ever had the kind of love you two have. For a love as powerful as what I'm witnessing right here, right now, yeah, maybe."

"I don't believe it for a minute," she countered. "You of all people know what it takes to get the kind of breaks we've had, to reach this level. You'd never throw it away, not for any reason."

He gave her sad look. "Yes, I would. For just one glance like the one you've been casting toward him, I'd walk away from anything."

It wasn't the first time that Gary had hinted that he was half in love with her himself, but he'd long since accepted that her heart belonged to someone else. He leaned down now and pressed a brotherly kiss to her cheek.

"Think about it," he advised. "We've known each other a long time. I can read you like a book. You'll never be thoroughly happy or alive if you don't find some way to keep that man in your life."

"But how?" she whispered as Gary walked away without answering.

How could she keep Harlan Patrick in her life and have a singing career, too? If she made a choice, either choice, would she be able to live with it, or would resentment destroy whichever one she chose?

No sooner had Gary left than Harlan Patrick rose with the baby in his arms and came back to join her.

"I think it must be close to lunchtime for the little one," he said quietly. "She's been fussing for a few minutes now."

"I'll fix her bottle," Laurie said, glad to have something to do.

"I liked the song," Harlan Patrick said as she heated the baby's milk.

"It's still a little rough, and the last verse sucks."

He grinned. "You're never happy till it's perfect, are you?"

"Of course not."

"You know, it seems to me that perfection might be fine to strive for when you're writing a song, but it's not real practical when it comes to life."

Her hand stilled as she reached to take the bottle from the microwave. "Meaning…?"

"There might not be a perfect solution to our dilemma."

She sighed, accepting the truth of that. "But there has to be something better than what we've come up with so far, don't you think?"

"Darlin', I'm not even sure what we've come up with, unless you count you being on the road and me being in Texas and both of us being miserable. That's not a solution. That's settling for the easy way out."

"It hasn't been easy," she objected.

"Okay, not easy. Convenient, then. Or maybe cowardly. Neither one of us has had to make any tough choices. We haven't even considered compromise."

She grinned at him and pressed her hand over her heart in a gesture of shocked disbelief. "I never thought I'd hear that word cross your lips."

He grinned back. "It's a new one, all right. You game to discuss it?"

"Oh, Harlan Patrick, can't you see? Discussing it's easy. It's living it that's impossible."

His jaw set. "Anything's possible if we both want it badly enough."

Pretty words, Laurie thought, but that's all they were: words. Their history told another story. It was Harlan Patrick's way or no way.

With Amy Lynn's future at stake, to say nothing of her own happiness, she would meet him halfway, though. "We'll talk about it," she promised.

"When?"

"Tonight, after the show. You can take me out to a late supper, since tomorrow's not a travel day."

"Why, Laurie Jensen, are you asking me out on a date?"

"I am," she agreed. "And I hope you've got your credit cards, because my tastes have gotten a whole lot more expensive. You're not going to get away with a hot dog and some cotton candy."

"Steak and champagne?"

She nodded. "For starters."

"Exactly where do you go next and when do you have to be there?"

"Ohio and not till the middle of the week. Why?"

"Just wondering," he said, and excused himself.

"Where are you going?" she demanded.

He gestured toward his seat. "Not far. I've got some arrangements to make."

"What kind of arrangements?"

"You'll see."

She didn't like the gleam in his eyes one little bit. Nor was she crazy about the way he and Val had their heads together for the next half hour whenever he wasn't on his cellular phone. Something told her she'd started something when she'd agreed to have dinner with him to talk about the future. He seemed to have taken it as a challenge. And just as he'd said earlier, one thing she knew for certain about Harlan Patrick was that the man did love a challenge.

Chapter Seven

Harlan Patrick knew he was taking a huge risk even as he made the plans for his first date with Laurie in years. He had no idea how she'd react when she discovered they weren't going out for a simple postperformance dinner.

For the first time in his life, he was truly grateful for the financial resources at his disposal. He discovered that money could make a lot happen in very little time. The hardest part was trying to explain to his uncle why the plane he had just sent back to Texas needed to be piloted right back out again.

"Harlan Patrick, are you sure you know what the devil you're doing?" Jordan inquired with an impatient edge to his voice. "I held my tongue when you took off with the corporate jet without a word to me. I sent my pilot to Montana to retrieve it without a single complaint. And now you want him to pick you up? I'm not running a blasted air shuttle. If Laurie's got you this tied up in knots, maybe you ought to get back home and think things over.''

"In a way that's just what I intend to do," he said, taking the well-deserved criticism without flinching. He knew he'd tested Jordan's patience to its limits, but he was also counting on the fact that his uncle still had at least a tiny touch of the Adams love of romance in his soul. After all, the tales of Jordan's elaborate attempts to convince Kelly to marry him were legendary. The current generation had made use of a few of them.

"Meaning…?" Jordan asked.

"I'm coming home and I'm bringing Laurie and the baby with me."

Silence greeted that announcement, followed by a sigh. "Are you sure that's wise? You know the kind of questions you're likely to face here, the pressure from your grandfather to marry."

Harlan Patrick matched his uncle's sigh. "I know, but I can't think of any other way to make her remember what we had. I want her to see what we could have again, if only she'd be reasonable."

"I sympathize with the position you're in, I really do, but I seem to recall that Laurie's got a mind of her own, to say nothing of a temper. This is a whole lot more complicated for her than you're making it out to be. The fact that you're saying she's the one who needs to be reasonable tells me you don't fully understand her position."

"Dammit, I do know it's complicated," Harlan Patrick replied.

"Do you really? It seems to me your first mistake was not taking her seriously enough years ago. Are you absolutely sure you can see her point of view now?" He waited, then asked, "Or are you just trying to bulldoze right on over her the way you always did?"

Harlan Patrick wasn't entirely comfortable with the question. He supposed he did have a tendency to get a notion into his head and then run with it, regardless of the other person involved. Some might say he was selfish and bullheaded. He preferred to think he was simply fighting for what he believed in.

"You haven't answered me," his uncle persisted.

"Dammit, we have a baby," Harlan Patrick retorted. "That's what's important. Not my feelings or Laurie's. I want that baby to be a part of my family."

"Well, of course you do," Jordan soothed. "But tricking Laurie into coming back to Texas when she's made it clear she doesn't want to be here seems like the wrong way to go about it. Why not just ask her to come?"

"What makes you think I'm tricking her?" Harlan Patrick grumbled defensively. "Maybe I have asked her."

"Then why are you whispering? That's a surefire indication that she's close by and you don't want her to know what you're up to."

"Maybe it's just a surprise. What's wrong with that?"

Jordan chuckled. "Depends on whether it's the sort of surprise the recipient will appreciate. Not all of the surprises I tried out on your aunt Kelly went over that well, as I recall. You know," he added thoughtfully, "there are some similarities. My business was in Houston then, and Kelly wanted to stay right here in Los Piños on her ranch. We fought about it tooth and nail for a while."

"And you were the one who gave in. Okay, okay, I hear you," Harlan Patrick conceded reluctantly. "Are you saying you won't send the plane back? If you are, I understand. I'll arrange for a charter."

"Forget chartering another plane," Jordan said impatiently. "I can just imagine what your grand-daddy would have to say if I did that. If you need the plane, it's yours. You let me know what time you want the pilot ready to bring you back here, and he'll be waiting at the closest airstrip."

"Thanks, Uncle Jordan."

"Don't thank me yet. I'm still not convinced you're not making a huge mistake."

When Harlan Patrick hung up, he tried very hard not to think about his uncle's reaction. What if Jordan was right? What if Laurie was infuriated by his scheming? What if this plan of his backfired?

But how could it? He was just trying to assure that Laurie remembered the good times, so she could weigh them against what she had now.

He glanced around at the lavishly appointed custom interior of her touring bus, then recalled the club date she'd played the night before with its standing-room-only crowd and wild applause. How would a quiet stay in Los Piños stand up against that? Would it be a welcome respite or a stark contrast that couldn't measure up? What about the men she'd met? Were they more exciting than a simple rancher from Texas?

"How are those plans coming?" Val asked, leaning across the aisle and breaking into his gloomy thoughts. "Everything falling into place?"

"Pretty much. Thanks for going along with this and for agreeing to come to Texas with us." He studied Laurie's assistant with her short blond curls and deceptively innocent expression. No one knew better than he just how fiercely loyal and efficient this woman could be. "Tell me something, Val."

"If I can."

"Is Laurie going to go through the roof when she figures out what I have in mind?" It bothered him more than he wanted to admit that this comparative stranger might know Laurie—today's Laurie—better than he did.

Val grinned. "Very likely."

He winced. "Why doesn't that seem to bother you?"

"Because she needs shaking up. She needs to take a long hard look at her priorities. She's got a handsome man—the father of her baby—absolutely wild about her and she'd rather sing songs to strangers night after night."

She gave him a solemn look. "Now don't get me wrong. I'm not saying she shouldn't sing if it matters to her. Millions of people would go nuts if she even thought about quitting. I'm just saying she needs to get some balance back in her life. She seems to think it has to be one way or the other.'' She tilted her head and regarded him quizzically. ''Wonder where she got an idea like that?''

Harlan Patrick sighed. ''Probably from me.''

''You still feel that way?''

He searched his heart and had to admit that a part of him did still want her home with him a hundred percent of the time, especially now that they had a daughter. For all of his crazy and impulsive exploits, it seemed he was just an old-fashioned guy at heart.

''You do, don't you?'' Val guessed without him saying a word. ''No wonder the two of you butt heads. You've both got a mile-wide stubborn streak, don't you?''

''Maybe so,'' he conceded. ''But I'm working on it.''

She looked skeptical.

''I am.''

''I hope so, but we'll see, cowboy. We'll see.''

Laurie was exhausted by the time she left the stage after her last set. It was ironic, really. She'd reached a point in her career when she could perform for an hour or ninety minutes before thousands in the country's biggest concert halls and stadiums and she'd chosen to do twice that much singing in clubs that could barely hold a hundred.

But these were the clubs that had given her a break. When she'd been a struggling nobody, these out-of-the-way club managers had offered her a chance to hone her act and build a following, and she believed in paying back old debts. She could have insisted on a single seating, just one show a night, but she wasn't about to shortchange either the clubs or her audience. She did two performances nightly and she sang her heart out.

By the time she retreated to her dressing room after the second show, she wanted nothing more than a hot shower, something cold to drink and a good night's sleep. Instead, she found Harlan Patrick waiting for her, straddling a chair just the way he had been when she'd first discovered him in her dressing room the night before.

Had it only been twenty-four hours since he'd walked back into her life? It felt as if he'd been back forever, stirring her up, making her long for things she'd resigned herself to never having.

"You look all done in, darlin'."

"Now, that is just what a woman wants to hear," she grumbled as she sank onto the chair in front of her mirror and methodically wiped off her stage makeup. "If you can't say something nice, go away."

"Have you forgotten? We have a date."

She groaned. She had forgotten. Well, almost forgotten. It was pretty much impossible to forget entirely about Harlan Patrick and his expectations.

"Not tonight, please. I was awake most of the night, thanks to you. I'm exhausted. I'll be lousy company. All I want is a good night's sleep."

"You could never be lousy company. Besides,

you promised me an evening out,'' he reminded her. ''Don't worry. You'll have time to catch a little cat-nap on the way.''

Her gaze narrowed at the gleam in his eyes. ''On the way to where?''

''Dinner, of course.''

She met his gaze in the mirror, didn't like what she saw and turned around. ''What are you up to, Harlan Patrick?''

''Just think of it as living out a fantasy.''

''Oh, no,'' she protested. ''I don't like the sound of that.''

He grinned. ''Everybody has a fantasy, darlin'.''

''Yes, but yours and mine can sometimes be worlds apart.''

''Trust me.''

She was troubled by the soft-spoken plea. Harlan Patrick had a way of asking her to trust him, then leading her straight into a whole mess of trouble. He'd been doing it forever.

There'd been more than once when he'd lured her out her bedroom window to go skinny-dipping in the creek out at White Pines. There'd been the time he'd insisted they both needed hot-fudge sundaes at midnight and broken into Dolan's to get them. When they'd been caught, he'd counted on Doc Dolan's high tolerance for Adams shenanigans to get them out of the fix they were in. Heck, he'd even told her he had protection the night Amy Lynn was con-ceived and he had. It was just that their passion had outlasted his supply.

"Harlan Patrick, read my lips," she said quietly. "I do not trust you."

He seemed stunned by her response, but as always, his eternal optimism and supreme self-confidence kicked in. "Give it time, darlin'. You did once and you will again."

"You make it sound so simple."

"It is simple."

"No, it's not. It has never been simple between the two of us."

That square-cut Adams chin jutted up in defiance. Blue eyes challenged her. "We've loved each other forever. What could be simpler than that?"

"We've also broken each other's hearts. If you ask me, that complicates things."

His expression wavered just a little at that. "Okay, you have a point. Let's not try to solve everything in one night. You'll come with me tonight, have a nice dinner, some quiet conversation and we'll see where it leads."

He made it sound so easy, so nonthreatening, when his very presence in her life was a danger. With his glib tongue and determination, he could make her believe in anything, even the two of them.

"I don't know, Harlan Patrick. Another night would probably be better."

His eyes caught hers, held. "Please."

In all the years she'd known him, she couldn't remember him ever using that word before. With strangers, maybe. His family, definitely. But not with her. With her he teased. He cajoled and coaxed.

He commanded, but a simple *please* had always seemed beyond him.

In the end that was what got to her. It hinted at his desperation, maybe even at his willingness to change if that's what it took to get her back.

"Okay," she said finally. "I did make a promise. But it can't be a late night, Harlan Patrick. Val's with Amy Lynn now, but I can't ask her to baby-sit half the night. She already works way too hard."

"Deal," he said at once. "Now, shake a leg, darlin'. We've got places to go, things to do."

"In the middle of nowhere?" she said, shooting him a wry look in the mirror. "We'll be lucky if there's a fast-food restaurant open."

"I can do better than fast food," he assured her. "You just wait and see."

Harlan Patrick packed while she finished dressing. She hid a grin at the sight of him folding everything and tucking it into her bag in nice, neat piles. She would have been satisfied to stuff it all in helter-skelter and worry about the wrinkles later. The man did have a thing about neatness, especially when it came to clothes. Except when he worked, his were always impeccable. His blasted jeans had precise creases in them. It was just another contradiction between them.

"All set?" he asked when he was finished.

She regarded him with amusement. "I've been ready. You're the one who's been dillydallying over the packing. What is this obsession of yours with neatness?"

He scowled. "It's not an obsession. If you have things, you take care of them. That's all."

"Did that come from your father and grandfather teaching you to take care of the ranch?"

"The ranch, family, whatever."

They were waltzing close to dangerous territory now. Laurie regarded him cautiously. "In other words you protect what's yours?"

"Something like that."

She concluded there was a point that needed making. "Clothes are one thing, Harlan Patrick. I'm another. It's not your job to protect me."

"I think it is. You and Amy Lynn are my responsibility," he insisted emphatically. "Just because you ducked out on me and hid Amy Lynn for months doesn't make it less so now that I've found you."

She winced at his stubborn expression. "Forget it. I am not having this conversation with you, not tonight."

"Wise decision," he commented as he ushered her out of the club and into a waiting car. "It's an argument you can't win. Now just sit back, close your eyes and rest till we get where we're going."

"Oh, no," she retorted. "I'm not closing my eyes or turning my back on you for one single second, Harlan Patrick Adams."

He grinned. "Suit yourself."

But despite her vehement protest, Laurie felt her eyes drifting shut within a matter of minutes. Lulled by the car's motion, she was sound asleep in no time.

When she eventually awoke again, she had no idea how much time had passed. Her eyes snapped open as she realized that the sound she was hearing couldn't possibly be a car's engine. One glance around confirmed that she was riding in an airplane—Jordan's corporate jet, unless she was very much mistaken.

"Harlan Patrick!" she bellowed when she didn't spot him right away.

He poked his head around the back of her seat. "Hush, darlin'. You're going to wake the baby."

"I'm going to do more than wake the baby," she threatened. "I am going to wring your sneaky, conniving neck, right before I toss you out of here. Where are we and where are we going?"

"We're in a plane."

"That much is clear."

"Jordan's plane."

She sighed heavily. "I thought so. I thought you'd sent it back to Texas."

"I had."

"Your uncle must be thrilled with all the use his jet is getting these days."

"Let's just say he's resigned to it."

"Let's move on to the other question I asked. Where are we going?"

He met her gaze evenly. "Home, darlin'. We're going home."

Laurie felt her heart begin to thud dully. "Home," she repeated in disbelief. "You've kidnapped us and you're taking us back to Texas?"

"I haven't kidnapped you," he insisted, looking offended.

"What would you call it?"

"You agreed to come to dinner. I picked the place. Mine."

"I'm in the middle of a concert tour. I can't go to Texas," she protested.

"Of course you can," he contradicted. "You told me yourself, you have a couple of days off before you're due in Ohio. We'll fly up day after tomorrow. The band will meet you there."

"And you took care of all these little logistical details yourself?" she asked skeptically.

He looked vaguely uneasy. "Not exactly."

To Laurie's astonishment, Val popped up just then.

"I helped," she announced unrepentantly.

"You?" Laurie asked incredulously. "Might I point out that I am the one who pays your salary. I'm the one who should be giving the orders."

Val grinned. "You pay me to make things happen. I made this happen."

"But I didn't want this to happen," Laurie all but shouted.

"Sure, you did, darlin'. You just didn't know it," Harlan Patrick responded in a low, soothing tone. "Don't blame Val. It was my idea."

"Oh, I am very sure of that," she agreed. "I'll deal with you in my own good time."

Despite the threat and her scowl, apparently he concluded it was safe enough now that the initial explosion was over, so he slid into the seat next to her. She glared at him. He smiled right back at her.

"I ought to hate you for this," she said.

"But you don't," he said confidently. "Do you?"

"I'm still debating."

"Laurie, face it. You couldn't hate me if you tried. Not really."

"You know, Harlan Patrick, one of these days someone's going to come along and bring you down a peg or two. Not everyone finds your inclination to control things amusing."

He chuckled at that. "Maybe so, but it won't be you."

"Don't count on it," she said grimly. "This little jaunt may prove to be just the incentive I needed to change my ways where you're concerned."

She folded her arms across her middle, settled back in her seat and prepared to endure the rest of the trip. As she stared out the window into the inky black sky with its dusting of stars, she reached a decision. Harlan Patrick might have won this battle with his clever little scheme, but the night wasn't over yet. She could turn the tables on him when they landed. In fact, she had the perfect scheme in mind.

A half-hour later they were on the ground at the tiny Los Piños airstrip. Harlan Patrick had a car waiting for them. Laurie gazed into his triumphant eyes and felt a moment's unease. He was going to be really, really unhappy when he realized what she intended.

So what? she consoled herself. He was the one who'd dragged her back here without asking. He was the one who was so hot to recapture the past. She'd take him back a few years, all right. Right down memory lane. There was one person on earth who'd never been charmed by Harlan Patrick, one person who'd been able to keep him in his place.

She turned and regarded him innocently. "Swing by my mom's, okay?"

"Now? It's the middle of the night."

"She's never seen Amy Lynn," Laurie explained, keeping her tone innocent.

"She can see her in the morning," he countered.

"Indulge me."

"Oh, for heaven's sakes," he muttered, but he turned the car toward town.

There wasn't a lot of sight-seeing to be done between the airstrip and Los Piños and it was too dark to see anyway, but with every mile they covered, Laurie felt herself drifting back to another time in her life. She was a teenager again, and a reluctant Harlan Patrick was driving her home from a date.

He pulled into her mother's driveway just moments later, and Laurie got out, along with Val and the baby. Harlan Patrick followed, feet dragging now that he'd lost control of events.

"You're going to scare her to death turning up here like this," he warned as Laurie rang the bell, rather than using the key she still had in her purse.

"Whose fault is that?" she countered.

Lights began coming on all through the house as her mother made her way to the door. Then it was open, and her mother's bemused, worried expression turned to pure joy when she saw the little crowd on her doorstep.

"Hi, Mama," Laurie said, walking into her tearful embrace. "I'm home."

"Oh, you beautiful child, come in here. Come in here right this minute. And you must be Val. I've heard so much about you. Now let me see that precious granddaughter of mine," she said, reaching for Amy Lynn and taking her from Val's arms.

"Oh, my, she is beautiful," she whispered. "She reminds me of you when you were a baby, Laurie."

Her gaze fell on Harlan Patrick then, and she beamed at him, too, obviously feeling more benevolent toward him tonight than she usually did.

"You did this, didn't you? You brought our girl home again. I can't thank you enough. You just carry her bags right on up to her old room and don't pretend you don't know which one it is, because I remember all too well how many times you climbed that tree outside her window."

Harlan Patrick stared at her, clearly flabbergasted by the unexpected turn of events. "But—" he began.

"Go on, Harlan Patrick. Do as Mama said," Laurie said, shooting him a triumphant grin.

"This isn't what was supposed to happen," he muttered under his breath.

Her grin widened. "No, I'm sure it isn't."

He scowled at her. "You will pay for this, darlin'."

"I'm sure you'll try to see to it that I do," she agreed. "You might want to remember, though, that when it comes to being sneaky, I learned from a master."

Chapter Eight

She had bamboozled him! Harlan Patrick drove out to White Pines still cursing the fact that Laurie had actually managed to trump him at his own game.

He couldn't very well stand in Mrs. Jensen's living room and demand that Laurie, Amy Lynn and Val leave with him. For one thing the woman was so clearly ecstatic about having her daughter home again. For another, Mary Jensen was no pushover. She had very strict ideas about morality. She would have managed to shame him for even thinking of taking Laurie to his home, when the two of them weren't married. Never mind the fact that they had a little girl as proof that their relationship had ventured beyond hand-holding.

Oh, Laurie was a sneaky one, all right. She had

known just what would happen when she walked through that front door. She had also known that he would indulge her whim to stop by, because he had always given her everything she'd ever wanted.

She would pay for it, though. She would pay the minute he could think of something devious enough to get the upper hand again.

A half-hour later he walked into his small house on a far corner of Adams land and slammed the door behind him. The thud gave him a moment's satisfaction, but he wouldn't be truly satisfied until he had his daughter and Laurie under this roof with him.

If there'd been any choice at all, he would never have left them in town where they were free to sneak off the instant his back was turned. He'd just have to trust that Mrs. Jensen would be no more anxious than he was to let them go or that Val was strong-willed enough to rat out her boss if Laurie got a notion to run. That was an awful lot of blind faith for a man who'd had some lousy lessons in broken trust lately.

He sank down on the sofa, too exhausted to even bother with taking off his boots or hauling himself up to bed. Besides, he'd had too many very erotic images the past couple of days of Laurie being back in that bed with him to want to climb into it alone.

Why did he have to want her so damned much? Life would have been a whole lot less complicated if his daughter were the only one who mattered to him. He could battle to get custody of her and forget all about her mama.

But that wasn't possible. He might have been furious with her, but one look at Laurie up in Montana and he'd known that he was going to have to fight tooth and nail for both of them. He was as captivated by Laurie as he'd ever been. She enchanted him as much as she infuriated him, a mix that had been dangerous to a man forever.

Anger, rage, betrayal all paled beside the white-hot need to hold her in his arms again, to bury himself deep inside her and hear her cries of pleasure mounting with every thrust of his body. Images hot enough to singe burned behind his eyelids and kept him restless.

When daybreak came, he hadn't slept a wink. He was in no mood at all for the pounding on his door that had him dragging his butt off the sofa.

"All right, all right," he muttered as he yanked open the door to find his father on his doorstep.

"So, you are here. Your mother told me she'd seen you come flying by in the middle of the night," Cody Adams said, scowling at him. "I told her she had to be wrong, that it must have been one of the hands coming in late. Aren't you supposed to be in Montana with Laurie?"

"It was four o'clock in the morning," Harlan Patrick grumbled, ignoring the reference to Laurie. He figured they'd get back to her soon enough. "What was Mom doing up?"

"She never sleeps well when one of her chicks is far from the nest. She figures Sharon Lynn has Cord looking out for her now, so she can concentrate on you."

"Heaven help me," Harlan Patrick said fervently.

His father grinned. "You could go a long way toward settling her down if you brought Laurie and Amy Lynn back with you. Are they here? Did you convince them to come home?"

"More or less. I'm surprised Uncle Jordan didn't fill you in."

"What does that mean? What does Jordan know that I don't?"

"It means I pulled a fast one to get them back here and they wound up in town with her mother," he admitted reluctantly.

His father's infamous grin broadened. "Not what you had in mind, was it?"

"No. That woman's sneakier than Grandpa Harlan."

"I doubt that," his father said. "You'd better hope he hasn't gotten wind that Laurie's back or he'll be meddling in your life, too."

If turning the matchmaking over to his grandfather would have worked, Harlan Patrick was just about desperate enough to try it, but he wasn't prepared to admit that to his father.

"I haven't spoken to Grandpa Harlan since I left," he said.

"But Laurie has," his father reminded him. "He told me all about it. That conversation got his hopes for the two of you up real high, and that was before he found out about the baby."

"He knows about Amy Lynn?"

"Oh, yeah. We tried to stop it, but that tabloid

has made the rounds. Janet finally decided it was pointless trying to keep it from him.''

''How'd he take it?''

''Needless to say, he'd be down here himself building a nursery, but Janet won't let him do it since he came close to breaking a hip the last time he climbed up on a ladder. Don't be surprised, though, if a whole crew shows up here later today with lumber and baby supplies. You know your grandpa once he gets a notion into his head.''

Harlan Patrick studied his father intently. ''For a man who recently claimed he didn't like Laurie, that she wasn't good enough for me, you seem mighty amused by all of this.''

''It's your opinion of her that counts. As for me, I'm reserving judgment on Laurie for the moment. Meantime, I have to admit, there's nothing I like better than watching your granddaddy stir things up. Keeps him young.''

Despite the levity, something in his father's voice stirred alarm. ''He's okay, isn't he?'' Harlan Patrick asked.

''He's fine. You know your grandfather. He's a stubborn old cuss. He'll probably outlive us all, especially if there's another grandbaby or great-grandbaby he feels the need to see settled in life. You're his number-one project these days, so consider yourself warned.'' His expression sobered. ''You planning on coming back to work today? We could use the help.''

Guilt washed over Harlan Patrick. He'd left the ranch in a bind when he'd taken off, though his father had been gracious enough not to belabor the point. Still, he couldn't just get back on his horse and ride off on some chore when his whole damned life was so unsettled.

"Never mind," his father said before he could reply. "We'll manage. You won't be worth a hoot to us as long as Laurie's on your mind. Just do me one favor."

"What's that?"

"Stop by the house and see your mother. She's worried about you. Has been ever since you took off. She and Sharon Lynn were carrying on the night you left, blaming themselves for your going, for letting you get a glimpse of that picture. She won't rest easy till she sees with her own eyes that you're doing okay."

"I'll go by for breakfast on my way into town," Harlan Patrick promised.

"That'll make her happy. She'll start the waffle iron the minute I tell her. From the day she married me and stopped working at Dolan's, she's happiest when she's serving up a big breakfast. If we hadn't had you kids, she would probably have taken over that lunch counter the way Sharon Lynn has done."

"Surely you're not complaining," Harlan Patrick teased. "Seems to me nobody likes breakfast better than you, especially when you get a chance to sneak a kiss whenever Mom passes by the table. Better than sugar, you used to tell us."

His father grinned. "It was and is."

"Spare me the details," Harlan Patrick replied. "Just tell Mom to make those waffles blueberry."

"As if she'd make anything else but your favorite when she's feeling a need to baby her youngest." He put his hand on Harlan Patrick's shoulder and gave it a squeeze. "You bring those gals of yours by when you can. I have to admit, I'm a little anxious to see my granddaughter, too."

"I'll have 'em out here just as soon as I can," Harlan Patrick promised.

It was one vow he intended to keep before the end of the day. Whether he could get them to stay, though, was another matter entirely.

Harlan Patrick consumed a plateful of waffles and let his mother fuss over him for the better part of an hour before he insisted on getting into town to check on Laurie. The minute he was out of sight of the house and his mother's watchful eyes, he hit the accelerator and drove into town at a pace all but guaranteed to have the local sheriff on his tail. Fortunately the local sheriff was his cousin Justin. He grinned when he saw the flashing lights behind him.

"Dammit, Harlan Patrick, you keep driving like that and I won't have any choice except to give you a ticket," Justin grumbled. He waved his citation book under Harlan Patrick's nose before stuffing it back in his pocket. "Where's the fire?"

"I'm going to see Laurie."

His cousin's expression turned sympathetic. "Ah, I see."

"I don't see why you say it like that."

"Because you never knew any way to chase after Laurie except full speed ahead."

"And the problem with that would be...?"

"She always knows exactly what to expect. In fact, she probably counts on it."

Harlan Patrick didn't like what Justin was suggesting. "Are you talking in general here or are you referring to that tabloid picture?"

"It is possible she planned it," Justin mused. "Who'd know better how to plant publicity designed to catch your attention?"

"She was trying to block the baby from view. Anybody could see that."

"She didn't do a very good job of it, though, did she? That baby of hers was in plain view."

"You're spending too much time around the criminal element. You're starting to see conspiracies everywhere you look."

"I'm just saying the woman had to know that you'd come hightailing it after her, the minute you saw that picture." Justin regarded him intently. "She was expecting you, wasn't she?"

"Of course not," Harlan Patrick retorted, then thought of all the roadblocks Laurie had put in his path. Half of Nashville had been warned to keep her whereabouts secret. "Okay, she assumed I'd come running, but she didn't want to be found. In fact, she did everything she could to see that I couldn't find her."

Justin gave him a pitying look. "Oh, please, Harlan Patrick. Who knows better than Laurie how you respond to a challenge. The more difficult she made it for you, the more determined you'd be to track her down. That's your nature."

"Am I that predictable?"

"You are where Laurie Jensen is concerned. Maybe you ought to think about being the one to turn your back this time. Let her do the chasing."

The idea held a certain appeal. Unfortunately he and Laurie weren't the only ones whose fate was at stake. "You're forgetting about Amy Lynn."

"No, I'm not. It is precisely because of your daughter that I want to see the two of you get it right. Let Laurie find her way back to you, Harlan Patrick. Maybe she needs a challenge in her life, too. If you don't believe me, just look at how hard she worked to become a superstar, when she could have done nicely as a singer right here in Texas. Every time you mentioned a roadblock to her back then, she found some way to scramble over it."

What his cousin said made a lot of sense, but Harlan Patrick pictured Amy Lynn, imagined losing her if he made the wrong decision. "I can't turn my back on them," he said finally. "I can't take that chance."

"I know it would be hard," Justin said sympathetically. Then his eyes lit up, and he grinned. "Remember that little bird we found when we were kids, the one that had fallen out of its nest?"

"Are you sure you're not confusing me with Dani? Your sister is the vet in the family."

"Think back. We were maybe five or six. We nursed that little bird for a week or more, fed it what seemed like a hundred times a day."

Slowly a dim memory began to take shape. "It

was a scrawny little sparrow, wasn't it? I kept wanting it to be a baby eagle.''

Justin's grin spread. "You were delusional. Anyway, remember when it was strong enough and Grandpa Harlan told us it was time to set it free? You'd gotten real attached to that bird by then and didn't want to let it go. You said you loved that little bird, and it loved you."

It all came back to him then, the feeling of panic that had come over him at the thought of letting the tiny creature fly away. "I remember," he said quietly.

"Do you also remember what Grandpa Harlan told us? He said when you love something, you have to let it go, that it's only when it comes back to you of its own free will that you can truly know the meaning of love."

The parallels to his current situation were obvious. Harlan Patrick sighed. "Quite a philosopher, our grandfather. He has a nasty habit of being right most of the time, too."

Justin grinned. "Don't look so downcast. Do you remember what happened with that sparrow once Grandpa Harlan convinced you to set it free? It came back and sang its little heart out for us all summer long."

Harlan Patrick's spirits lifted. "Yeah, it did, didn't it?"

"And the moral of this story is…?" Justin prodded.

"Okay, okay, I get it. You don't have to whack me over the head with it."

"Then I'll be on my way," Justin said. He'd walked only a couple of steps before turning back. "By the way, cousin. If I catch you going so much as one mile over the speed limit, there won't be enough money in the family coffers to bail you out of my jail."

Harlan Patrick laughed, which put a scowl on his cousin's face.

"I'm dead serious."

"I know you are. That's why it's so funny. You can lock me up and throw away the key, but I flat out guarantee you that granddaddy will have your badge for it. Weigh that while you're chasing me down."

He let that warning hang in the air as he put the car into gear and took off, kicking up a trail of dust just to taunt Justin. The man really did need to loosen up. He'd hoped marriage to Patsy would do the trick, but it hadn't. Therefore Harlan Patrick considered it his personal—if not his civic—duty to see to it.

Laurie expected Harlan Patrick to show up at her mother's again before dawn. When he still wasn't there by nine, she began to wonder what he was up to. As the morning dragged on with no sign of him, her gaze kept straying toward the window.

"Expecting someone?" Val inquired as she sipped another cup of coffee.

Val had settled into Laurie's mother's kitchen as if she'd been visiting there for years. She'd appropriated the portable phone to follow up on publicity arrangements for the final stops on the tour. She had papers spread all over the Formica-topped table. One thing Laurie had to say for her: Val could work efficiently just about anywhere. She didn't require the trappings of an office.

Val continued to regard her with amusement. "Not answering, huh? Must mean the answer's yes."

"Just how furious do you think he was when he left here last night?" Laurie asked.

"Who?"

"Who do you think?" Laurie growled. "Harlan Patrick was the only man who left here in the middle of the night, wasn't he?"

"As far as I know," Val said evenly. "I'm just surprised it matters to you. You seemed mighty anxious to see him go. You were looking downright pleased with yourself when he walked out the door."

"I wasn't anxious for him to go," Laurie protested. "I was just trying to make a point."

Val tried unsuccessfully to smother a grin. "Well, I guess you succeeded, then, didn't you? He knows now that you are even trickier than he is."

"Do you suppose I should call him?" Laurie fretted.

"If you want to."

"I don't want to," she snapped.

"You just said—"

"I'm just worried that something might have happened to him. It was awfully late. He was ticked off at me. He was probably driving too fast the way he always does. The roads out here are dark as sin. What if his car's in a ditch or something? Who besides us would know to go looking for him?''

"Worried about me, darlin'?" the very man in question inquired from behind her.

Laurie almost jumped out of her skin at the sound of his voice. She whirled around and glared. ''Don't you sneak up on me.''

"I thought you'd be relieved to hear my voice. Weren't you picturing me in a ditch?''

"With pleasure," she retorted.

His crooked smile mocked her. ''Liar, liar,'' he taunted.

"Well, you're just fine, aren't you, so it hardly matters what I was thinking.''

He gave Val a wink, then bent and brushed a light kiss across Laurie's lips. ''Glad to know you missed me.''

"I never said I missed you," she said, though an unmistakable shiver had washed through her at the touch of his lips against hers.

"Didn't have to," he said, helping himself to a cup of coffee. ''That blush tells the story.''

"I do not blush, Harlan Patrick.''

He cast a look toward Val. ''What do you say? Did her cheeks turn pink just now or not?''

Val held up a protesting hand. ''Leave me out of this. The woman pays my salary.''

"If she fires you, I'll hire you," Harlan Patrick promised. ''We can always use a whiz like you out at White Pines.''

Laurie tried to stop herself, but she couldn't help

it. She chuckled at the image of the dainty whirlwind before her herding cattle. "Somehow I don't see Val on a ranch. Getting up close and personal with a cow is not her style."

"We have an office, darlin'. We have books to keep, logistics to plan. Something tells me Val could grasp the details in no time."

"But she'd hate it," Laurie countered. "Val likes the world of country music, don't you, Val?"

"All that singing about heartache and cowboys and you don't think she'd like to meet the real thing," Harlan Patrick retorted before Val could reply. "I say we take her on a tour and let her decide for herself."

Laurie's gaze narrowed. "This is just your sneaky way of getting us out to White Pines, isn't it? You're just itching for the family to get a look at your daughter."

"Well, of course I am," he agreed. "Nothing says we can't include a little sight-seeing for Val along the way."

"Val has things to do."

Harlan Patrick turned to her assistant. "Is that right? Are you too busy to pay a visit to the ranch?"

Val heaved an exaggerated sigh of relief. "Finally. I am so glad that somebody noticed I was still in the room." She shot a defiant look toward Laurie. "And I would absolutely love to see the ranch." She stood up. "I'll get Amy Lynn ready to go, if I can pry her away from your mama, that is."

She scooted out of the room in the blink of an

eye, leaving Laurie alone with the most impossible man on earth.

"How is it that you have managed to twist that woman around your finger already?"

"Charm, darlin'. It used to work on you, too."

"That was before I knew you better."

"You really are going to have to do better than that, if you intend to insult me."

She regarded him curiously. "You really do let my barbs roll right off your back, don't you?"

"Most of them," he agreed. His expression sobered. "Not all."

"Funny," she observed. "I never thought I got to you at all."

"Except by leaving," he said quietly. "You knew that one was a real killer, didn't you?"

Laurie was startled by the genuine pain in his voice, the flash of vulnerability in eyes that normally twinkled with mischief. The accusation stung because it implied that she'd gone only to hurt him.

"I didn't leave to make you miserable, Harlan Patrick. Surely you've figured that out by now. Or do you still think my music is some clever little game I play, a nasty habit you're forced to tolerate?"

He sighed and raked a hand through his hair. "No. I know how important your music is. I ought to. You've chosen it over everything else in your life."

She frowned. "I won't have this conversation with you again. It never changes. You try to make me feel guilty for loving what I do. I blame you for trying to take it away from me, for making me choose. What's the point, Harlan Patrick? We always end up right back where we started.''

''Amy Lynn's the point.''

''Amy Lynn is doing just fine with the things the way they are.''

''Now, maybe,'' he conceded grudgingly. ''She's a baby. What happens when it's time for her to go to school? You planning on dragging a tutor along on tour with you? Or do you intend to shuffle her off to some boarding school?''

''For heaven's sakes, Harlan Patrick, it'll be years and years before she goes to school,'' she protested impatiently. ''When the time comes, I'll make whatever arrangements are necessary.''

''What about friends? How's she supposed to have friends if she's always on the go? A kid needs a home, roots, family, just the way you and I did.''

''You had that, not me,'' Laurie countered. ''I had a mother who struggled every day of her life to keep a roof over our head. That's it. Talk about living with insecurity. Been there. Done that.''

She stared at him defiantly. ''And I survived. It certainly wasn't the same as you living all safe and secure out at White Pines, surrounded by family.''

''All the more reason why you should want what I had for Amy Lynn.''

''Who knows better than I do that you can get by with less?'' she countered, even though the truth was that not a day of her youth had gone by that she hadn't envied what Harlan Patrick had. Not the

money so much, but the ranch and what it repre-
sented—history and family.

"And that's what you want for Amy Lynn?" he
inquired softly. "Less than the best?"

"That is not what I meant," she said, shoving her
chair back and leaping to her feet so she could pace
in the small kitchen. He was twisting her words,
trying to instill enough guilt so she would cave in
and let him have his way. Once he would have gotten away with it, too, but she was stronger now,
tougher and smarter. She could see right through
him.

"That's what you said," he insisted.

"Only because you make me so crazy I don't
know what I'm saying half the time," she said,
pausing to glower at him. "Besides, thanks to my
career, I can provide Amy Lynn with all the financial security she'll ever need and then some. We
don't need you."

That claim was meant to rile him, and it did. His
eyes glittered dangerously. She tried to make a clean
getaway, but he snagged her hand as she whirled
around. Before she knew it, he'd hauled her into his
lap.

"Let me up," she demanded, shoving ineffec-
tively at his chest.

"Not till you admit I'm right," he said, a teasing
sparkle replacing the fury that had put fire in his
eyes only seconds earlier. "Not till you admit you
need me."

"When hell freezes over," she retorted.

"Admit it," he commanded.

"Never."

"Say it or I will…" His gaze clashed with hers, held. The silence built. Tension shimmered in the air.

"Or you will what?" she asked, her voice suddenly shaky.

"This," he whispered just before his mouth claimed hers.

His fingers tangled in her hair as he coaxed her lips apart. His tongue dipped, tasted, savored. Then hers did the same. The kiss stirred her blood, stirred memories. He tasted of coffee and just a hint of maple syrup. Laurie rocked back in his lap and grinned.

"Your mama made you waffles this morning, didn't she?"

"What if she did?"

"The woman spoils you rotten. No wonder you're so impossible."

"I'm not impossible, darlin'." He shifted her ever so slightly so she could feel the hard shaft of his arousal. "When I'm with you, I am always very, very possible."

She sighed and buried her face against his shoulder, relaxing into the wondrous sensation of having his arms tight around her again. Last night, walking into her mother's house again after being away for so long, had been incredible, but this? This was what it felt like to come home.

"Oh, Harlan Patrick," she murmured. "If only everything were as easy as you make it sound."

"It's as easy or as complicated as we make it."

"Then why do we insist on making it so complicated?"

"Damned if I know," he said ruefully. "Maybe that's just how it has to be, so we'll appreciate what we have when we finally work it out."

She pulled back and gazed into his eyes. "I hope you're right. I really do."

He smoothed her hair back from her face and smiled, a sad, wistful little smile. "I hope so, too, Laurie. I truly do."

Chapter Nine

A knot of dread formed in Laurie's stomach as they got closer and closer to White Pines. Once this ranch had been like a second home to her. She and Harlan Patrick had explored every acre of it on day-long horseback rides and picnics. She'd been welcome at family gatherings, included on special occasions, all because everyone had assumed that one day she and Harlan Patrick would marry.

She wondered what they thought of her now. Oh, she knew what Harlan Patrick had told her, that everyone, including his grandfather, cared only that she'd given him a daughter. That might be what they told him, but she had little doubt that resentment would be simmering below the surface. How could it not be? He was an Adams, and she had betrayed him.

Hands clenched, she stared out at the rugged, familiar terrain and tried to see the beauty in it that Harlan Patrick saw, tried to feel the same connection to the land. All she felt was uneasiness and the same restless urge to wander that had driven her away from Texas years ago.

As much as she loved the people here—as much as she loved one particular person here—it hadn't been enough. She had desperately wanted a singing career. She had needed to be somebody, on her own, not just because she married into the wealthiest family in town. Marrying a man like Harlan Patrick would have been blind luck, not an accomplishment she could claim.

"You okay?" Harlan Patrick asked, giving her a sideways glance as he turned into the long driveway leading up to the sprawling house that had been built as a replica of the home his Southern ancestors had lost in the Civil War, then recreated after moving west.

"Sure."

As if he could read her mind, he said quietly, "Nobody here hates you, Laurie."

"Then why do I feel as if I'm on my way to my own hanging?"

"Don't go blaming me for that," he said less sympathetically. "I'm not accountable for whatever guilty thoughts you're having."

She scowled. "I have absolutely nothing to feel guilty about."

"Then stop agonizing over what's to come.

You're going to visit a few old friends, show off our beautiful daughter. What's the big deal?''

"The big deal is that I kept Amy Lynn from you. Don't you think I know how that will make me look in everyone's eyes, especially your sister's? Sharon Lynn and I were friends once, but when I walked out on you, it changed things between us. This will only make the tension worse.''

He braked to a stop on a curve in the lane and faced her. "The only person whose opinion really matters here is me, Laurie.''

"Okay, then,'' she said, accepting the truth of that. "What about you? Have you forgiven me?''

He hesitated at the direct question, then sighed. "No, but I'm working on it.''

That sinking sensation returned to the pit of her stomach. "Thanks. That really helped,'' she said sarcastically.

He reached over and touched her cheek. "I love you just the same as I always did. The rest will come.''

In the back seat, Val cleared her throat loudly. "Excuse me for interrupting, you two.''

"What?'' Laurie and Harlan Patrick asked in a startled chorus.

"Don't look now, but there are several huge beasts ambling this way. Is that significant?''

Harlan Patrick glanced in the direction Val indicated and chuckled. "They're just cows coming to see what's going on over here. They're hoping we might be planning to drop some feed over the fence.''

"And if we don't?" Val asked, eying them warily.

"They'll wander away."

"No retaliation? No stampede?"

Laurie laughed at her assistant's vivid imagination. "You almost sound disappointed. Were you hoping for a tale of danger you could repeat all over Nashville?"

"Sure," Val said with a nervous chuckle. "It would be great publicity, you know." She paused, her expression thoughtful, then added, "As long as you don't get trampled."

"Yeah," Laurie said dryly. "That would be a bummer."

"Everybody settled down and ready to move on now?" Harlan Patrick asked.

"More than ready," Val replied.

"As ready as I'll ever be," Laurie said grimly.

In the back Amy Lynn gurgled and waved her tattered stuffed bear in enthusiastic agreement.

"I guess that's everybody, then," Harlan Patrick said, watching his daughter in the rearview mirror, his expression amused. "Okay, baby girl, let's go home."

His tone was lighthearted but the statement was laden with hidden meanings that immediately put Laurie on edge all over again. This was not Amy Lynn's home. Her home was hundreds of miles away in Nashville. She wondered, though, if there was anything she could say or do to get that through Harlan Patrick's thick skull.

* * *

Harlan Patrick bypassed the turn that would have taken them to his own home or his parents' and headed straight for White Pines itself. He'd called his mother from Laurie's and told her to meet them at the main house. He figured it would be easier on everybody if there was one big welcome, rather than having to go through reunion after reunion, especially when some were bound to be uncomfortable.

Laurie's obvious case of nerves was beginning to get to him. He suspected even Amy Lynn could sense her mother's mounting tension. She'd begun fussing just as they reached the house, and nothing Val could do seemed to soothe her.

"I'll take her," Laurie said, leaping out the instant he cut the engine. She rushed around to the other side and practically snatched Amy Lynn from her car seat as if she needed to stake her claim before anyone else did.

"Planning to use her as a shield when you enter the enemy camp?" Harlan Patrick inquired lightly.

"I'm trying to get her to settle down," she countered defensively. "She probably needs changing, and it's almost lunchtime. We should have waited until another time to do this. I wasn't thinking."

"You've been doing that a lot lately," he observed.

Her eyes glittered dangerously. "What?"

"Not thinking."

She frowned. "Don't you dare do this," she warned in a low tone. "Don't you dare try to start something with me just as we're going in to see your family."

Was that what he'd been doing? More than likely, he was forced to admit. "Sorry. I didn't mean to make this any more difficult." He reached for the baby. "Let me carry her. She's too heavy for you."

Laurie held Amy Lynn a little tighter. "She's fine."

"Okay, then, let's go. Val, you all set?" he asked as she lagged behind them.

"I think maybe I should stay out here for a bit, maybe take a walk. I don't belong in there right now."

"Of course you belong," Laurie said at once. "You're my friend."

"And mine, too, I hope," Harlan Patrick said. "Though I can understand why you might prefer to stay out of the cross fire. If you'd rather go for a tour, I can get one of the hands to take you around."

She nodded eagerly at that. "Yes. That would be wonderful."

"Wait here. I'll see who's around."

As he headed for the stables, he saw the newest hire bringing a horse into the paddock. Slade Sutton was an embittered ex–rodeo star, barely into his thirties, who'd been brought aboard to work with the horses and to start a breeding program. With his taciturn demeanor Sutton wouldn't have been his first choice for tour guide, but Harlan Patrick suspected his choices were going to be limited at this time of day.

"Hey, Slade, you got a minute?"

The no-nonsense man scowled predictably at the

interruption and limped over. "Just about that. No more."

"I need you to do something for me," Harlan Patrick said, ignoring the man's testiness and his obvious reluctance to be drawn into any task that didn't involve the horses.

"What's that?"

"I've got a real tenderfoot out here who needs a tour. I wouldn't ask except the next hour or so is going to be tense inside and there's no need for her to be a part of that."

Slade's scowl deepened. "You didn't hire me to play tour guide. I've got horses to work with."

"Then let her watch. She'll be content with that, as long as you manage to throw a smile her way every now and again, along with an explanation of what you're up to. I'd be grateful if you'd help me out."

He walked off to get Val before the man could protest again. When he came back with her in tow, Slade didn't even bother to look up from his work until Harlan Patrick called his name insistently.

"Slade Sutton, this is Val Harding. She's Laurie Jensen's assistant."

There was a brief flicker of recognition and surprise at the mention of Laurie's name, but no more. Slade tipped his hat and went back to using his pick to clean the caked-up dirt in the horse's shoe.

"Slade doesn't say much, but most of what he does say is profound," Harlan Patrick told her, drawing a sour look from the man in question. "I'll be back for you when the fireworks are over."

"I'm sure I'll be fine," Val assured him, proving that she would rather be any place on earth than inside White Pines. She sent a beaming smile toward Slade. "I'm sure Mr. Sutton and I will get along very well."

Harlan Patrick was pretty sure he heard Slade mutter a contradictory response under his breath, but he let it pass. As cantankerous as he knew the man to be, he also knew he would never be overtly rude to a woman. Silent, maybe, difficult definitely, but not rude. Sutton prided himself on being a cowboy through and through, and basic courtesy was ingrained. It might be interesting to see how the ever cheerful Val handled him, but unfortunately he couldn't stick around to watch. He had his own awkward situation to deal with.

Naturally, by the time he walked back to the front of the house, everyone had poured into the yard and Laurie and his daughter were surrounded. She might have feared being cast as the bad guy, but at the moment she appeared more in danger of being smothered by eager Adamses, anxious to get a look at the newest addition.

"Hey, give the woman some room," Harlan Patrick called out. "Otherwise, she'll make a break for it the first chance she gets."

There was more truth than jest in his words, and everyone there seemed to know it. They backed off instantly, everyone except his grandfather. He stood his ground, his gaze on the little girl in Laurie's arms.

"She has Adams eyes," he noted with pride.

"And an Adams chin." He held out his arms. "May I?"

Laurie never hesitated. "Of course. Sweetie, this is your great-grandpa Harlan," she said as she handed the baby over.

"Oh, darlin' girl, I'll bet you are a handful," Grandpa Harlan said with tears shimmering in his eyes. "Come along with me and I'll tell you all about being an Adams, then I'll explain how I'm going to go about spoiling you rotten."

"Oh, no, you don't," Harlan Patrick's father contradicted, all but snatching the baby out of his arms. "That's my job now."

"Don't fight over her," Janet chided her husband and stepson. "Honestly, you'd think the men in this family had never had an heir before, the way they carry on over every baby."

"You're just mad 'cause you're not getting a turn to fuss over her," Grandpa Harlan retorted, linking arms with his wife. "Come on, everybody. Let's go inside, so we can be comfortable."

Laurie hung back as the others climbed the steps. Harlan Patrick lingered beside her.

"Feeling better now?"

She gazed up at him, and to his amazement there were unshed tears welling up in her eyes. "They love her," she whispered. "Just like that, she's one of them."

"Well, of course she is. No matter how things stand between you and me, she's my daughter. Did you think for one second they wouldn't accept her?"

"No, but…" Her voice trailed off, and she looked away.

"But what about you?" Harlan Patrick suggested quietly. "Is that what you were going to say?"

She nodded. "They barely even looked at me."

"Darlin', that's not a reflection on you. Haven't you been around this family long enough to know that any new baby stirs everybody up? The mom and dad tend to get lost in the shuffle until the novelty wears off. Would you have preferred it if they'd laid into you right off for hiding Amy Lynn away these past months?"

"No, of course not."

"Well, then, be grateful to our little girl for taking the heat off us for the moment."

"I suppose you're right."

"I know I am. Once the questions start, you're going to wish they were back to ignoring you."

She managed a shaky smile at the reminder. "I *know* you're right about that. By the way, how's Val?"

"I left her with an ex–rodeo star."

Laurie grinned. "That ought to make her day."

"It might if he ever says more than two words to her. Slade's not the talkative type."

"That's okay," she said with a grin. "Val is. She'll have his life story out of him before he can blink."

"Now, that would be worth paying to see. He's been here two months and none of us knows more than his rodeo history and his way with horses."

"We could sneak around back and watch," Laurie suggested, gazing wistfully in that direction.

"Oh, no, you don't. We belong inside, and inside is where we're going." He captured her hand in his and found it icy cold. "Still nervous?"

"Wouldn't you be if you had to face the inquisition I do?"

"I do have to face the inquisition you do," he reminded her. "I'm not off the hook here, sweetheart. I do know one thing that might take your mind off of it, though."

"What's that?" she asked suspiciously.

"This."

He lowered his head and settled his mouth across hers. If the kiss earlier had stirred temptation, this one set off skyrockets. Nothing on earth could fire his blood the way the simple touch of Laurie's lips could. The woman's mouth was magic, soft as satin and clever as the dickens. She could turn a nothing little kiss into pure sin.

By the time the kiss ended, he was sucking in great gulps of air and trying to ease the pressure of denim on a very sensitive part of his anatomy. Every shift in movement, though, was torture.

"I want you so bad, my whole body aches with it," he murmured against her ear as he held her loosely in his arms. "Maybe we could sneak away to my place."

"Not five seconds ago you were insisting we had to go inside," she reminded him.

"That was before."

"Before what?"

''Before I remembered what it was like to feel you up against me. You could drive a man crazy.''

''And that's a good thing?'' she asked doubtfully.

''Oh, yeah, that is a very good thing.''

''You were singing a different tune when you showed up in Montana. Chasing after me drove you crazy, and you weren't one bit happy about that.''

''We're talking about two very different things here.''

''Lust being one,'' she guessed. ''And the other?''

''Life, love, getting along, whatever you want to call it.''

She nodded. ''I think I get it now.'' With that she poked him sharply in the ribs. ''And I do not like it, Harlan Patrick. You're saying I make you crazy physically, so you want to sleep with me, but beyond that, I just plain drive you crazy.''

''More or less,'' he admitted, gingerly rubbing the spot she'd punched. ''Did you want me to lie about it?''

''That depends.''

''On?''

She grinned at him then. ''Whether you ever want to sleep with me again.''

''Oh, I do, darlin'. I surely do.''

''Offhand, I'd say your chances right now are about that of a snowball's in hell.''

With that she whirled around and marched up the steps and into the house, leaving him to ponder the wisdom of telling the truth over uttering a more diplomatic little white lie. Short-term, the truth clearly had its drawbacks. Long-term, well, that remained to be seen, he concluded as he followed her inside.

Laurie stood in the doorway to the living room and drew in a deep breath. Half the adults were down on the floor with Amy Lynn, who appeared to be ecstatic at all the attention. The child was showing off her first teeth in a grin that had everyone cooing at her. She crawled from one new relative to another and offered smacking kisses.

"Quite the little charmer, isn't she?" Harlan Patrick said proudly.

"Like her daddy," Laurie observed with less enthusiasm.

"Seems to me she's more like her mama, enjoying being the center of attention."

"Don't start with me, Harlan Patrick."

"That wasn't a jab," he insisted.

"Sounded like one to me."

He frowned. "Does every conversation we have have to disintegrate into an argument?"

"Seems that way."

"I'm tired of it, Laurie. I'm tired of the sparring. Aren't you?"

"Yes," she conceded.

"Then let's make a pact," he suggested. "Let's declare an honest-to-God truce. Let's promise to think before we open our mouths and try not to keep hurting each other."

"I'd be happy to go along with that, if you will."

"I will," he vowed solemnly, and sketched an X across his chest. "Cross my heart."

If only she could count on him remembering that promise for longer than a minute, she thought wistfully. Harlan Patrick always said what was in his heart. It was a blessing and a curse. She never had to sort through lies and evasions, but she also had to shield herself from the sometimes brutally painful honesty.

She studied his face intently, saw the sincerity in his eyes. "I promise, too," she said just as Harlan Adams spotted her.

"Laurie, my girl, come over here and sit beside me. We have some catching up to do."

"Badgering more than likely," Harlan Patrick murmured.

She grinned. "I can handle your grandfather," she assured him, then winked. "Can you?"

"Doubtful," Harlan Patrick conceded. "Let me know how it turns out."

"Oh, no, you low-down, sneaky cowboy. This re-union was your idea. You can come along and share the heat."

"Now, that sounds downright fascinating."

"I didn't mean it that way."

"You sure? Sometimes a slip of the tongue can be very telling."

She regarded him impatiently. "Try to drag your mind out of the gutter for two seconds and come with me. I am not facing your grandfather alone."

"I thought you said you could handle him."

"I can, but I want backup."

"Sorry. I left my shotgun at home."

"I doubt guns will be called for. Just use that

inimitable charm of yours to steer the conversation in some other direction if he starts asking about our intentions.''

Harlan Patrick gave her a worrisome grin. ''Why would I want to do that? I'm mighty interested in what you have to say on that subject myself.''

''Watch your step,'' Laurie warned. ''Or I'll tell him you'll be lucky if you're not dead by the time I head out of here tomorrow.''

On that note she headed across the room leaving Harlan Patrick to amble after her. She knew he'd come, if only to protect his own hide.

''Sit right down here,'' Harlan Adams said, patting the place beside him on the sofa. ''Boy, you can drag over one of those chairs since you evidently don't trust me to have a private conversation with your girl here.''

When Harlan Patrick was settled, his grandfather turned to her. ''Young lady, I have a bone to pick with you.''

Laurie tensed. ''What's that?''

''When you called here a few days ago, why didn't you say a word about that pretty little baby of yours?''

She breathed a sigh of relief. That was an easy one. ''I wasn't sure how much you knew, or how much Harlan Patrick knew, for that matter. I figured you'd say something if you'd seen the tabloid and put two and two together.''

He nodded knowingly. ''That's why you called, then? You were pumping me for information?''

''Afraid so,'' she admitted. ''I wanted to know if

Harlan Patrick had seen the picture and if so, what his mood was. You told me all I needed to know when you said he'd taken off for parts unknown.''

"You could have told me the truth, you know," Harlan Adams scolded.

"I didn't think it was my place," Laurie insisted. "I figured it was Harlan Patrick's news to share with his family when he saw fit."

"I suppose you're right," he agreed, then looked at his grandson. "So why didn't you tell me before you left town to go chasing after her?"

"When I left here, I was fit to be tied. All I was interested in was finding Laurie and getting at the truth myself," Harlan Patrick responded. "That's all water under the bridge now, Grandpa. The important thing is that Laurie and Amy Lynn are here now."

"For how long?"

"Until tomorrow," Laurie said, her chin lifted combatively.

"Tomorrow!" Harlan Adams exploded. "Why, that's no time at all."

"I'm in the middle of a concert tour. I wouldn't be here now if it weren't for the fact that your grandson virtually kidnapped me. I have a concert date tomorrow night in Ohio."

"And then?" the older man persisted. "Will you be back then?"

Laurie sighed. "No. There are a few more dates after that, and then I have to get back to Nashville to work on the next album."

Harlan Adams looked troubled. "I see. Your

mama must be disappointed by that as much as I am.''

"She's just pleased we got this unexpected chance to visit," Laurie said pointedly. "She wasn't well enough to travel when I had Amy Lynn, and since then I've been on the road so much, there was no point in dragging her along from city to city."

Harlan Patrick grinned. "And we should be grateful for stealing a few unexpected minutes with you, too, right?"

"Yes," she said succinctly.

"I have an idea," Harlan Adams said with a worrisome glint in his eyes.

"What's that, sir?"

"Why don't you leave Amy Lynn right here while you're off running around? It'll give us a chance to get to know her, and you'll have some peace of mind knowing she's well cared for while you're working."

Laurie was on her feet at once, trembling. "No, absolutely not," she said backing away. "Amy Lynn stays with me. She is my daughter. Dammit, I knew this would happen. I knew it." She glared at Harlan Patrick. "You put him up to this. I know you did."

She turned her back on the two men, crossed the room in quick, angry strides, plucked Amy Lynn off the floor and headed outside. After basking in all the attention, Amy Lynn was furious at the disruption. She began to wail as Laurie raced from the house with her clutched tightly in her arms.

Not until she was outside by the car, breathing

hard, did she finally stop. Forcing back her own hysteria, she tried to soothe her daughter.

"Shh. It's okay. I'm sorry, baby. I know you were having fun. I didn't mean to scare you."

She sensed Harlan Patrick behind her even before he spoke.

"You didn't have to take off like that, you know. A simple no would have sufficed."

"Really?" she asked, whirling on him. "When has a simple no ever meant anything to an Adams? You all scramble, scratch, claw, manipulate, whatever it takes to get your way. Just like I said in there, for all I know, you put your grandfather up to that."

Despite her vow to herself that she wouldn't cry, she felt the salty sting of tears in her eyes, even as fury and frustration mounted.

"You won't get her away from me, Harlan Patrick. You won't."

"I haven't tried, have I?" he asked reasonably. "That was Grandpa Harlan's idea, not mine."

"But you'd jump at the chance to keep her here if I'd go for it, wouldn't you?"

"Well, of course I would. She's my daughter, and I barely know her. What would a few days matter, Laurie? You could pick her up after the tour ends, or I could bring her back to you in Nashville."

"No," she said again, just as forcefully.

"Why not?"

"Because…"

She looked into the eyes of this man she had known practically her whole life, a man she had loved almost that long, and tried to gauge his intentions. She couldn't, not entirely, and because of that she voiced her greatest fear.

"Because I don't know if you'd ever give her back."

Chapter Ten

As Laurie's words cut through him, Harlan Patrick had to fight the urge to shake her. How could she ever imagine that he would talk her into leaving Amy Lynn with him and then refuse to give their daughter back? How could she accuse him of even contemplating such an underhanded thing? Did she think he was capable of pulling a low-down, dirty stunt like that? Did she think he would sink to her level? That was what she had done, after all. She had kept his daughter from him. He should have thrown that in her face just to see how she liked it.

Instead, because she was holding his daughter in her arms, he battled with himself until his temper was under control, then said evenly, "If I say I will bring her back to you, then that's what I will do,

Laurie. Have you ever known me to go back on my word?''

Her cheeks flushed. ''No,'' she conceded. ''But the circumstances have never been like this before, either. I guess what I'm saying is that I almost wouldn't blame you if that's what you did. Isn't that exactly what I did to you?''

He was surprised by her admission, reassured somehow that she recognized the irony of the accusation she had leveled at him.

''Yes,'' he said mildly. ''But the time for casting blame and getting even is over. What we have to do now is figure out the future and what's best for Amy Lynn.''

She seemed to clutch their daughter a little more tightly. ''What's best for Amy Lynn is not to have her life disrupted. She's always been with me. What would she think if I just vanished, even for a few days? I don't want her thinking I abandoned her. I know what that's like all too well.''

''Let Val stay, too. That would give Amy Lynn a sense of continuity. It might also reassure you that I won't be able to get away with stealing her right out from under you. Val would have my hide first.''

''I can't,'' she protested. ''I need Val with me. There are endless details she needs to see to when I'm on tour. I'd be lost without her.''

It was this intransigence that had kept them apart all these years. ''Come on, Laurie. Work with me. Compromise. Val is the queen of long distance. She can make things happen from anywhere. She doesn't have to be glued to your side.''

He could see from her expression that she was struggling with herself, wanting to do what was right and fair, but terrified of choosing wrong.

"I'll think about it," she said finally. "That's the best I can do."

"Talk to Val. See what she says," he urged.

"This isn't about Val, dammit. It's about Amy Lynn," she said as she struggled to hang on to the increasingly restless baby.

Harlan Patrick forced a smile for his whimpering, frustrated daughter, then met Laurie's gaze evenly. "It's also about trust, isn't it? It's about whether or not you really trust me to keep my word."

"Yes," she agreed.

"I never broke my word," he reminded her. "You did."

And then he turned and walked away before he said a whole lot more, before he lashed out with bitter words he might never be able to take back.

Gently bouncing Amy Lynn in her arms, Laurie stayed where she was and watched Harlan Patrick leave. Funny, she hadn't realized just how badly it hurt to be left behind, to have the person she loved turn his back on her. Sure, this was only an argument, a faint blip on the canvas of their relationship, but she felt as empty and lost as if he'd gone for good.

Was that how he'd felt when she'd gone? Or had it been a thousand times worse, knowing that she had no intention of coming back again? She realized suddenly that it hadn't been the same for her.

Though she had missed Harlan Patrick desperately, especially in the first months after leaving, she had been excited by the future, challenged just to survive. She had been moving on, while he had stayed behind.

"Everything okay?" a feminine voice asked gently.

Laurie turned from the direction in which Harlan Patrick had gone to find his mother standing quietly behind her.

Melissa Adams was a fiercely protective woman who loved her husband and children with all her heart. She had also been strong enough to stand up to Cody Adams years earlier and refuse to marry him even though she had his child—Sharon Lynn—until she knew for sure that Cody truly loved her. In some ways her circumstances back then were not unlike Laurie's now. The difference was that Cody was the one who'd left Texas not knowing that he was about to become a father, while Laurie had walked away from Harlan Patrick.

"I suppose it depends on your definition of *okay*," Laurie said wearily. "He's furious with me."

"Because you don't want to leave your daughter behind tomorrow when you go?"

"That, and because I left in the first place, because I wouldn't marry him years ago and settle down as a rancher's wife."

"You did what you had to do," Melissa Adams stated.

Laurie stared at her in surprise. "You can see that?"

"Well, of course I can," she said with a hint of impatience. "He put you in a terrible position by forcing you to choose."

"I never wanted to make that choice," Laurie added. "It was like having to decide whether to keep my right arm or my left."

Melissa smiled at the analogy. "I imagine it was."

"I always thought we could work it out. Foolish me," Laurie said. "I knew the man was stubborn, but I also thought he loved me enough to want what was best for me."

"Come over here and sit with me," Melissa said, leading her to a grouping of chairs in the shade of a tree. "You have to understand something about Harlan Patrick. As hard as his daddy and I tried to avoid it, he grew up knowing that the world was his for the asking. You can thank his granddaddy for that. Harlan thinks the sun rises and sets on his family. It doesn't mean he doesn't see their flaws. Goodness knows, he does. He just leads each and every one of them to believe he can have it all. When it doesn't work out that way, it's always a huge surprise."

She chuckled. "You should have seen Cody's face the first time I told him no. You'd have thought I hit him with a two-by-four."

Laurie found herself grinning. "I can imagine."

"Harlan Patrick took it even worse when you said no," Melissa said quietly. "It came close to breaking my heart to see him hurting so. I hated you for that, but that doesn't mean I couldn't see that you were doing what you needed to do. You have a gift from God with that voice of yours. It's your right, maybe even your duty, to do what you can with it, to see how far it can take you."

"I need to sing," Laurie said, grateful for even this much understanding. She tried to explain why that need was a match for her love for Melissa Adams's son. "I need to know that I'm good enough, that I can stand on my own two feet. My mother never had that. Once my father walked out, every single day of her life was a struggle. I never wanted to be that dependent on anyone. Music seemed to be the answer. If I hadn't had a decent voice, I would have chosen something else, but I would have had a career of my own."

"Have you ever explained that to my son?"

Laurie paused thoughtfully, realizing that she'd always just assumed he knew. "Not in so many words, no."

"Maybe you should."

"It wouldn't change anything. I'd still have to go, and he'd still have to stay."

"But at least he'd understand that you're not just leaving him. Tell him, Laurie. Don't let him go on thinking that he's the one who's not good enough."

Laurie was shocked by Melissa's words. "Not good enough? How could he possibly believe that?"

"Because you left him behind." She regarded Laurie sympathetically. "If you go again and take his daughter, you'll just be adding to his sense of failure. You'll be telling him you don't think he's good enough to be a daddy, either. Please, Laurie, talk to him. Do whatever you think is right about Amy Lynn, but talk to Harlan Patrick.''

Laurie squeezed the older woman's hand. ''I will. I promise. It was never my intention to make him think he wasn't good enough. It was about me and what I needed.''

''Let me take Amy Lynn back inside, then, and you go find him,'' Melissa suggested. ''The two of you need some time alone together to make peace.''

After a moment's hesitation, Laurie shifted Amy Lynn into Melissa's waiting arms.

''Take all the time you need,'' the older woman said. ''She'll be fine with us.'' She gazed straight into Laurie's eyes. ''And she'll be right here whenever you come looking for her. I promise.''

''Thank you,'' Laurie whispered in a choked voice. ''Not just for taking Amy Lynn. For this talk, for understanding, for everything.''

''You're more than welcome. Remember, it's my son's happiness that's at stake here, too. I have a vested interest in the outcome.''

Melissa headed toward the house, then turned back. ''I suspect you'll find him down by the creek. It's where he always goes when he needs to think.''

Laurie smiled. ''I remember.''

The creek was close enough to walk to, far enough away to give her time to think. Unfortunately it could have been at the ends of the earth and it wouldn't have been far enough for her to reach any conclusions about what she should do about the future or even about leaving Amy Lynn behind for a few days.

She'd spotted Val out by the paddock, engaging in a one-sided conversation with the rodeo star. Amused, she had concluded that her assistant very well might not mind being left behind along with Amy Lynn. She could use a new challenge in her life, a personal challenge, rather than the logistical kind Laurie presented her with every day. It was evident from her nonstop chatter in the face of his unsmiling demeanor that Val considered the cowboy a challenge.

Even so, Laurie wasn't sure she could walk away from her baby even for the few days remaining in the tour.

So, she concluded, she would continue to weigh the option, just as she had promised Harlan Patrick she would. In less than twenty-four hours she would have to make her decision. Something told her it wouldn't come any sooner, either.

As she reached the stand of cottonwoods along the edge of the creek, she spotted Harlan Patrick, leaning back against the trunk of one of them, his Stetson tilted down over his eyes. Even in repose, there was a tension evident in the set of his shoulders, in the grim line of his mouth.

She eased up beside him and settled down on the ground just inches away.

''You asleep?'' she inquired when he didn't move so much as a muscle.

''No.''

''Thinking?''

"Not if I can help it."

"What, then?"

"Trying to blank it all out, trying to pretend that you and I haven't come to this."

"Pretending doesn't help much, does it?"

"It might if it worked," he grumbled. "Can't say it's ever worked for me."

She thought of what his mother had said and made up her mind to tell him everything that had driven her away from Los Piños, away from Texas, away from him.

"Can I tell you something?"

He tilted his hat brim up and slanted a look at her. "I'm not going anywhere."

She tried to find a starting point, but had to go back a long way to find it. "Do you remember when my daddy left?"

He regarded her with surprise. "Your daddy? No, I can't say that I do."

"I do, Harlan Patrick. I remember it as vividly as if it were yesterday, and I was only four years old at the time. He and my mama fought that night. I could hear them from my room, the loud, angry voices, bitter accusations that I couldn't understand. To this day I don't know what the fight was about, just that it ended everything. When it was over, the front door slammed and, just like that, he was gone right out of our lives. He never came back." Hot tears welled up, then spilled down her cheeks. "He never even said goodbye."

Even now the memory was enough to make her ache inside. Loneliness and fear all but swamped her, but as bad as it was, all these years later it was only a sad echo of how terrible it had been back then.

"I'm sorry," Harlan Patrick said. "You never talked much about him."

"I couldn't. It hurt too much." Swiping angrily at the tears, she glanced over and met his gaze. "But you know what hurt even more?"

"What?"

"Watching what it did to my mama, what it did to our lives. We never had a secure day after that, not financially, not emotionally. I was always terrified that she would leave the same way he did, out of the blue, when I least expected it. I was scared that we'd run out of money and be thrown out of our home. And you know what else that did to me? I vowed then and there that I would never, ever be in that position."

"You had me, Laurie. You knew I would never desert you, that you'd always have everything you ever wanted."

"That was later. Besides, don't you see, my mama thought that about my daddy once, too. Look what happened to them. To me that meant that the only person you could really count on was yourself. That's why I went to Nashville. That's why I fought so hard to make it as a singer. I didn't leave you, Harlan Patrick. I went after the dream of what I could be, what I *needed* to be to make the fears go away."

He reached for her then, gathered her into his

arms. "Oh, baby, why didn't you ever tell me this before?"

"I did. At least, I thought I had. I thought you knew everything there was to know about me. It wasn't until today that I realized that it wasn't a fair assumption."

"I should have known," he agreed softly with her head tucked against his shoulder. "I should have been able to see into your heart."

"Maybe neither one of us understood that even between the closest of friends, sometimes you have to say the words and not leave anything to chance." She reached up and touched his face, tracing the familiar angles and planes. "I love you, Harlan Patrick. Please, don't ever doubt that. I loved you then and I love you now."

As she spoke, she felt the splash of a teardrop against her fingers and realized that her brave, fiercely strong cowboy was crying. "Oh, Harlan Patrick," she whispered brokenly. "Don't. Please, don't cry over me."

"Darlin', I never cry," he said, his voice husky.

Smiling at the predictable denial, she rose to her knees and knelt facing him. She cupped his cheeks in her hands, then brushed her lips across the salty dampness on his skin. When she claimed his mouth, he moaned softly, then dragged her against him, his hands swift and sure as they roved intimately over her.

Like a summer brushfire, need exploded between them. Memories that needed refreshing responded to each caress as if it were new. His touch was impatient, inflaming her with its urgency. With her breath already coming in ragged gasps and her blood racing, she clasped his hands and held them tightly.

"Wait," she pleaded.

He stilled at once, but there was torment in his eyes as they clashed with hers. "Wait?"

"Slow down. That's all. Just slow down. It's been a long time, Harlan Patrick. I want to savor every second."

He grinned and reached for her again. "Couldn't we hurry now and savor later?"

"Oh, no," she said, slapping away his hands, then reaching for the buttons on his shirt. "You just sit still and leave this to me."

That drew a spark of interest. "Leave it to you, huh? Sounds fascinating." He locked his hands behind his neck and relaxed back against the tree. "Do your worst, woman."

She chuckled. "Oh, I promise you, it will be very clever and it will be my best, not my worst." The first button on his shirt popped free, exposing a V of bare flesh with just a hint of wiry dark hair. She pressed a kiss to the spot, noticing that his skin was feverishly hot already. The pulse at the base of his neck leaped.

"Promising," she assessed, grinning at him.

The next button opened and then the next, exposing more and more of that wide, sexy chest for her increasingly inventive kisses. Oh, how she had missed this. She had missed the tenderness, the laughter and intimacy, the sensual games that only two people who loved and trusted could play.

When she reached the last button above his belt buckle, she tugged the remainder of the shirt free, then dropped a daring kiss on the bared skin where dark hair arrowed down toward the evidence of his arousal. He jolted at that and clasped her shoulders tightly.

"Careful, sweetheart. You're starting to take risks."

"I thought you were a man who liked to live on the edge."

"Not me. I'm just a stay-at-home, old-fashioned kind of guy."

With her fingers already at work on his buckle, she hesitated at the description. It cut a little too close to reality, when she was trying to recapture the fantasy.

"Need some help with that?" he asked, obviously unaware of the alarms his words had set off.

She drew in a deep breath, then shook her head. "Nope. I've done this before, you see."

"Not with anyone else, I trust," he said lightly.

She lifted her gaze to meet his and realized that despite the joking tone, the question was dead serious. "Never with anyone else," she said softly. "Only with you, Harlan Patrick."

There were plenty of men in her new world, record-company executives, fans, actors. She had thought about some of them, wished she could fall in love with one of them, wished she could want them as she wanted the man she'd left behind in Texas, but Harlan Patrick had always been right there in her head and in her heart. She sang about one-and-only loves a lot, because she had found hers years ago.

"Only with you," she repeated as she slowly slid down the zipper of his jeans and reached for him.

At the glide of her fingers across his arousal, he gasped and reached for her wrists, cuffing them with a grip that stilled any movement.

"Okay, darlin', you've had your fun," he said. "Now it's my turn."

"But I was just getting started," she protested, laughing at his refusal to leave her in control.

"And now I am," he countered.

Before she knew it, he had flipped her over until she rested beneath him on the soft, sweet grass. Somehow he managed to keep her hands neatly immobilized above her head, while his free hand began its own magical journey over fabric, resulting in chafing caresses that left her skin sensitive and burning. He didn't waste time on finesse. When he wanted to touch bare skin, buttons popped, scattering everywhere. Her bra clasp was dismissed as easily, and then his tongue was soothing the very skin he'd inflamed only seconds before.

Her nipples ached with the pleasure of it, and that was even before he took each one into his mouth and sucked, sending waves of delight rippling through her. Her hips, pinned to the ground by the weight of him, bucked ever so slightly, causing yet another delicious friction.

"We've still got on too damned many clothes," Harlan Patrick murmured in frustration, freeing her

hands so he could use both of his to dispense first
with his own clothes and then hers.

When she was naked, the soft, sultry breeze
kissed her skin and made her nipples pucker just as
his touches had.

"You are the most gorgeous creature God ever
made," Harlan Patrick said, his heated gaze studying her as if she were brand-new to him.

"I have stretch marks," she protested.

"From carrying my baby," he said, touching the
faint white marks on her belly with gentle reverence.
"That only makes you more beautiful."

She grinned. "How could any woman not love
you? You always know the right thing to say."

"I always tell the truth," he insisted.

"Truth or the view through rose-colored glasses,
I appreciate it," she said.

Even though she was the one who'd urged a
slower pace, she reached out to stroke him in a gesture guaranteed to shock him into action.

"Now who's impatient?" he taunted.

"Please, Harlan Patrick, make love to me. Make
love to me now."

"With pleasure, darlin'. With pleasure."

With the wicked skill of someone who knew her
body intimately, he skimmed touches over perspi-
ration-slick flesh, then dipped into the moist folds at
the apex of her thighs, finding the tiny nub that sent
her off into rippling waves of ecstasy.

Only then, when she was still trembling in the
aftershocks, did he part her legs and ever so slowly
enter her. The reunion was a stunningly sweet re-

minder of the past, a swirl of present-tense sensations and then an urgent journey into the future.

Past, present, future—love was there for all of it, making the throbbing tension and exquisite release seem unique to this moment, even as it echoed a haunting familiarity and held the promise of unending repetition.

Curved securely into Harlan Patrick's arms, Laurie wanted to believe in now and forever. She wanted the fantasy to last, but in no time at all reality intruded.

"Marry me," Harlan Patrick whispered, his hand resting against the curve of her breast, his voice thick with need. "Marry me, Laurie."

This time it was her tears that fell, splashing against his bare skin as her heart split in two yet again.

"I can't," she said, her voice choked. "Haven't you heard anything I've said? It wouldn't work."

"How can you say that? We're perfect together. We've always belonged together."

Icy cold and trembling, she pulled away and began frantically gathering her clothes, yanking them on with haphazard abandon until she was dressed, but still quivering in front of him. When she couldn't get her blouse closed because of the missing buttons, he silently handed her his shirt. She put it on, then tied the ends with trembling fingers.

"Explain it to me, Laurie. Tell me why it won't work, when we're so good together."

"Like this, we're perfect together," she agreed. "But the rest?" She gave an impatient, all-encompassing wave of her hand. "It hasn't changed, Harlan Patrick. I'm going back on tour tomorrow and you're staying here."

His mouth firmed into a grim line. "I'll get used to being separated."

"You won't."

"Then I'll come along."

"You'd hate that even more. And before too long, you'd hate me, too." She bent down and touched his lips one last time. "You know I'm right. In your heart, you know it."

Scooping up clothes, she left before he could counter that, but she'd gone only a few paces when she realized that he hadn't even tried.

Chapter Eleven

Harlan Patrick was mad enough to tear the whole blasted ranch apart, to say nothing of what he'd like to do to Laurie. How could the woman make sweet, passionate love to him one second and then walk away from him the next? It was insulting, demeaning.

Then again, he ought to be used to it. She'd done it often enough to be downright skilled at it, and he ought to be smart enough by now not to be taken by surprise.

While he wrestled with the black mood she'd left him in, he took his time walking back to the main house. Even though he had no desire to face Laurie again anytime soon, he had every intention of sticking as close as possible to his daughter. If Laurie refused to relent and leave Amy Lynn at White Pines while she finished her concert tour, then he was going right back on the road with her. It gave him a great deal of satisfaction to know that she was really, really going to hate that.

He was almost back to the main house when he crossed paths with one very surly, out-of-sorts Slade Sutton.

"Keep that woman away from me," the hand said, squaring off in front of him defiantly.

Even with his own problems fresh in his mind, Harlan Patrick couldn't stop the grin that tugged at his mouth. "Problems with Val?"

"She never shuts up." Slade scowled. "Next time you invite somebody out here who needs baby-sitting, get somebody else. I'm here to work with the horses. You decide to change the job description, I'm outta here."

There was little doubt he was serious about it, too, Harlan Patrick concluded. Val must have proved herself to be a real handful. Trying not to let his enjoyment of the situation show, he said, "I figured you'd be so used to breaking fractious horses that one little old filly wouldn't give you a moment's trouble."

"She's not a horse. She's a blasted nuisance," Slade growled, and stalked away.

Harlan Patrick hooted as he watched him go. "Made quite an impression, did she?" he commented under his breath. "I'll have to see what I can do about getting her back here."

He chuckled at the devious schemes already forming in his mind and concluded that there was a whole lot more of his granddaddy in him than he had ever realized. Matching the cantankerous former rodeo star with Val had been a stroke of genius. In fact, it might be the only good thing to come out of this whole damnable trip to White Pines.

In the midst of his laughter, he paused thoughtfully. If Val had a reason to want to spend more time in Texas, she was exactly the kind of woman who'd find a way to make it work. And if *Val* could make it work, wouldn't Laurie begin to see the possibilities, as well? It was something that bore thinking about, he concluded, and he would do just that, right after he made sure she hadn't stolen his pickup and hauled his daughter back into town or straight on up to Ohio and her next concert date.

To his relief he found Laurie inside, Amy Lynn sound asleep in her arms. The two of them were still surrounded by family. Val had joined them at last but was sitting by herself on the fringes, clearly trying to remain unobtrusive. Harlan Patrick went over and pulled a chair up beside her.

"How'd your tour of the ranch go?" he inquired innocently.

She shot him a wry look. "What tour? I could tell you exactly how long it takes to clean a horse's hooves. I could tell you exactly what shade of red Slade Sutton's neck turns when he's given a compliment. I could even tell you how much feed each horse gets. All of this is from my own personal observation, by the way. Mr. Sutton doesn't have a lot to say. And beyond the stables, this place remains a mystery.''

That was pretty much what Harlan Patrick had expected. ''And Slade?'' he inquired.

''What about him?'' she asked with a telltale touch of color in her cheeks.

''Does he remain a mystery?''

''Pretty much.'' She slanted a curious look at him. ''What do you know about him?''

''Probably not much more than you.''

''He works for you. Didn't he come with a resumé?''

''Of course, but believe me, it was very succinct and focused almost exclusively on what he knows about horses. In the end those were the only qualifications we cared about.''

''How'd he get the limp?''

''A rodeo accident, I suppose. As long as he can do the job, I saw no point in probing into how it happened. Besides he's made it clear he doesn't want to talk about it.''

She grinned at that. ''He doesn't want to talk about anything.''

''You didn't let a little thing like that put you off, did you?''

''Of course not. I considered it my duty to try to get one entire sentence out of him, something beyond *yup* and *nope,* that is.''

''And did you?''

''Eventually.''

''What did he say?''

'''I'm going to the bunkhouse now,''' she re-

ported, then sighed. "Not exactly what I'd hoped
for."

Harlan Patrick chuckled. "He didn't invite you
along, did he?"

"Oh, no. He all but shoved me toward the main
house." Her eyes sparkled with indignation. "I
could have been insulted."

"But you weren't?"

She shrugged. "It takes a lot more than that to
rattle my chains. It just made me more curious."

"Too bad you don't have longer to try to figure
out what makes him tick," Harlan Patrick suggested
slyly.

She gave him an amused, knowing look. "Oh,
something tells me I'll be back here before too long.
And when I am, Slade Sutton doesn't stand a
chance. I haven't run across a challenge like that
man in a very long time."

Bingo, Harlan Patrick thought triumphantly. He
glanced over toward Laurie and found her gaze on
him. She looked away at once, but not before he
caught the bleak expression in her eyes.

What on earth was she thinking? he wondered,
then realized he'd caught her looking at him just that
way on the tour bus when he and Val had been
huddled together making the plans for this trip. Was
it possible that she was jealous of the friendship he
and her assistant were forming? Surely not.

Then again, if she was, if she didn't grasp even
now how totally and thoroughly committed he was
to her, maybe he could make the insecurity work to
his advantage, too.

He settled back and pondered how to go about it. Maybe he should make a point of inviting Val back to White Pines for a visit in Laurie's hearing. Val wouldn't mistake the invitation for anything other than another chance to try to unravel the mystery of Slade Sutton, but Laurie? Who knew what she might make of it? Maybe it would shake her if she thought there was a chance she was going to lose him to a woman who had no hesitations at all about making the same choice that Laurie herself refused to make.

Was the plan devious? Of course. Would anybody get hurt? No one he could think of. Was it risky? Wasn't just about everything?

But on the chance it could work, it was a gamble he was more than willing to take. He intended to get Laurie to realize that they were meant to be together, no matter what it took, no matter how many obstacles had to be overcome. He just prayed his imagination was up to the task.

Tired of the pointed questions being asked about her plans for the future, Laurie broke free from her conversation with Sharon Lynn and went in search of Harlan Patrick, praying she wouldn't find him off somewhere with Val. She had no idea what sort of bond those two had formed, but she wasn't crazy about it. They'd already hatched up one kidnapping scheme. Who knew what they would come up with next.

She found Harlan Patrick outside—alone, thankfully—and joined him.

"I'd like to get back into town," she said stiffly.

"I want to spend a little more time with my mother before we leave tomorrow."

He slanted a skeptical look at her. "Is that it? Or are you just anxious to get away from my family? Are they getting to you, Laurie? Are you beginning to feel guilty about keeping Amy Lynn from them and from me?"

"I've always felt guilty about that," she retorted candidly. "But I did what I thought was best at the time and, frankly, I'm sick to death of apologizing for it. What's done is done, Harlan Patrick. I can't change it, and I won't let you use it to blackmail me into giving you your way."

"Is that what I'm doing?"

"Of course it is. You tried threats and that didn't work. You tried charm, and that didn't work either. You've even tried sex. Now you're letting your whole family gang up on me. I'm sick to death of it." Tears threatened, but she refused to shed them, blinking rapidly to keep her eyes dry.

He looked about ready to explode. "Do you honestly think that's why I made love to you?" He threw up his hands. "Forget it. Let's say that I did. Have you even once considered that I am trying all those things because this is too important for me not to use every weapon I can think of to get your attention?"

"It's not a war, dammit."

His gaze, as serious as she'd ever seen it, met hers evenly. "It is to me. I'm fighting to hold on to my family."

She swallowed hard at that, but she didn't relent.

She couldn't. "We're not your family, Harlan Patrick."

"Like it or not, darlin', Amy Lynn is my daughter. Around here that's about as close a family tie as you can have. I'll do whatever I have to, Laurie. My first choice would be to marry you, but you don't seem to want anything to do with that. Since that's the case, I have to consider my other options."

She regarded him worriedly. "What options?"

"I haven't settled on any yet. When I do, you'll be the first to know."

"Is that a threat of some kind?"

"You can take it any way you like."

She studied his intractable expression and sighed. "Have we really come to this?"

"Apparently," he said with evident regret. "Just remember one thing, Laurie. It was your choice, not mine."

She started to argue, but there seemed to be little point to going another round with him. He had his opinion about where the fault lay. She had hers. In the end it probably didn't even matter. All that really counted was that they were at an impasse. Again.

"Will you drive us back to town now? Or should I ask Justin? He and Patsy don't live all that far from my mom. I'm sure he'd love to have twenty uninterrupted minutes to get his two cents in. He's been scowling at me ever since he got here. Seeing that gun strapped to his waist and that badge of his gives me the jitters."

Harlan Patrick actually grinned at that. "It pretty

much had the same effect on me at first, but I'm getting used to it. I'm starting to enjoy tormenting him. As for giving you a lift, I'm sure he'd be delighted to, but there's no need. When the time comes, I'll take you."

He started to reach out, almost tangled his fingers in her hair, in fact, but then to her relief he drew back.

"We'll go right after dinner."

She balked at the delay. "I said I wanted to go now."

"We don't always get what we want in life, do we? You've certainly made up your mind to see that I don't."

"And this is payback?"

"Oh, no, darlin'. When payback comes, you'll recognize it right off. This is about my grandfather and the fact that he's already got the grill fired up and he's planning a big ol' barbecue to welcome you back into the fold. I don't want him to be disappointed."

If it was a ruse, it was a clever one. He knew she would never do anything to openly defy his grandfather's wishes. Harlan Adams had been too kind to her over the years.

"Fine," she said tightly. "After dinner, then."

"And just to show you that I am a reasonable man, I will have someone pick up your mom and bring her out here to join us. How about that?"

Relieved at the prospect of having an ally at last, she nodded. "That would be wonderful. Thank you."

"I'll go and make the arrangements, then."

She watched him go, hating that there was such tension and bitterness between them. Conversations were either stiff and awkward or they rapidly disintegrated into fights. Once they had shared everything, talked for hours, laughed together over the silliest things.

It had almost been easier before they'd made love. Now, knowing that the chemistry hadn't died, it was more difficult than ever to accept that love just wasn't enough.

"You still love him, don't you?" Val asked, joining her on the porch. "I can see it in your eyes."

"No, of course not," Laurie denied. "It was over a long time ago."

"Right. That explains why you came back here wearing his shirt and without a single button on your blouse. I saw it all knotted up and stuffed in your bag. That story about falling in the creek didn't quite ring true since your pants weren't the least little bit damp. I like the little midriff effect you tried so it wouldn't look quite so much like Harlan Patrick's shirt. Some people might never guess what happened. Of course, none of those people are inside."

Laurie groaned. "They know?"

"They're not blind. If the blouse hadn't been a dead giveaway, the color in your cheeks would have been." She studied Laurie intently. "Are you crazy? The man worships you. Why are you making things so difficult for him? Is there something I'm missing?"

"How many times do I have to explain that this

isn't about Harlan Patrick? For that matter, why do I have to explain anything to you? You work for me.''

The color drained out of Val's face. ''I thought I was also your friend,'' she said quietly. ''My mistake.''

She started to leave, but before she could go, Laurie caught her arm. ''I'm sorry. I didn't mean that the way it sounded. You know you're more than an employee. I don't know what I'd have done without you the last couple of years. You're the best friend a woman could ever have.''

''May I make a suggestion, then?''

''Of course.''

''You might want to get a lawyer.''

Shocked, Laurie stared at her. She could feel the blood draining out of her face. ''Why do you say that?''

''My impression of this family is that they fight fair, but they fight to win. Unless you and Harlan Patrick reach some sort of compromise about your daughter, I'd guess that he'll have you in court so fast, it'll make your head swim.''

''Has he said that?'' Laurie demanded. ''Is that what the two of you have been huddling about? Has he been making threats?''

''No, our conversations have been about Slade mostly.''

''Then why would you say something like that? How did he get you on his side?''

''I'm not on his side,'' Val said patiently. ''But Laurie, wake up. Face facts. You're keeping his daughter away from him. He's suggested you let her stay here while you finish your tour. You said no. He's asked you to marry him. You've said no.''

''How do you know all that?''

''I listen. In this crowd it doesn't take long for word to get around.'' She regarded Laurie intently. ''How long do you think it's going to be before he tires of taking no for an answer and sets his own agenda?''

The truth was he had already hinted at it more than once. She'd even asked him about veiled threats earlier, but he'd denied he was making any. ''What should I do?''

''Work it out. Be reasonable. Now, personally, if it were me and I had a guy like him that crazy about me, I'd be at the courthouse taking out a wedding license, but that's me.''

''He knows why I can't marry him,'' Laurie said defensively.

''No, he knows why you won't marry him,'' Val corrected. ''If you wanted to make it work, you could.''

When Laurie started to protest, Val held up her hand. ''Never mind. It's between the two of you. I'm butting out.''

''That'll be a first.''

''Well, it may not last, so be grateful for now.'' She grinned. ''As for me, I think I'll take a little stroll down by the bunkhouse.''

Laurie regarded her with amusement. ''Slade wouldn't be down there, by any chance?''

''Could be.''

"Since when do you go chasing after a man?"

"Believe me," Val said ruefully, "this one will not come chasing after me. I'm compromising. You might want to watch. It's easier than you think."

"Very amusing."

"I meant it to be instructive."

Val had walked about ten yards when Laurie realized that she was no longer wearing the sneakers she'd borrowed and put on earlier. She'd changed back to a more typical pair of slinky, totally inappropriate high heels. Laurie was pretty sure she knew why.

"Hey, Val, be careful. You're wobbling," she taunted.

"I am not wobbling. I've been walking in heels my entire life," Val called back.

"Not on a ranch. What happened to your sneakers?"

Val grinned. "They don't do nearly as much for my legs."

"I hope he's worth breaking your neck for."

"That remains to be seen."

Laurie watched her go, struggling between amusement and wistfulness. There had been a time when she had been just as giddy, just as eager to impress Harlan Patrick. For a little while earlier, she had recaptured that feeling by being in his arms again. All of those old yearnings had rushed through her, reminding her that once there had been a period of innocent belief that they could conquer anything.

As she walked back toward the house, she saw her mother emerging from a car along with Justin's wife, Patsy, and her son, Billy. Billy went racing off on sturdy little legs to join the other children crowding around their great-grandfather on the patio. Laurie went to meet her mother.

"Hey, Mom, I'm glad you came."

As Laurie linked arms with her mother, she smiled at Patsy, who appeared to be about fifteen months pregnant. "Thanks for bringing my mom out." Gesturing toward Patsy's huge belly, she asked, "When are you due?"

"Any day now, thank God. I'm not sure I'll be able to haul myself up out of a chair if I get any bigger. Justin's threatened to keep the town tow truck handy in case I get too big for him to manage."

"You should have seen me at nine months," Laurie said. "I felt like a blimp. I knew no baby on earth could weigh that much, which meant I was going to have a devil of a time losing the excess weight. Staying in seclusion meant I had way too much time on my hands to eat."

Laurie's mother interrupted. "I'm going to leave you two girls to talk about babies. I want to say hello to Harlan and Janet and thank them for including me."

She left before Laurie could protest. She glanced at Patsy, who was studying her enviously. She expected some sort of remark about her choice to stay in seclusion to keep her pregnancy a secret from Harlan Patrick.

Instead, Patsy said, "Obviously you didn't have any trouble with getting the weight off again. You're gorgeous. Practically skinny, in fact. How'd you do it?''

"I brought in a personal trainer and set up a gym. The man had no mercy.''

Patsy sighed. "Well, I'm afraid a trainer's out of the question on our budget. I guess I'll have to get back in shape the old-fashioned way, by chasing after the kids and starving myself to death.''

Laurie decided then and there that she would send her trainer on an extended trip to Los Piños as her baby present to Patsy. The man could work miracles in a month. Faster if he hated being stuck in what he was likely to consider the middle of nowhere.

"Don't worry about a thing," she told Patsy, making a mental note to have Val call the trainer in the morning and make the arrangements. "You'll do just fine. You did after Billy was born, didn't you?''

"I never got this huge with Billy. Will wasn't around the way Justin has been. Justin hovers. If I don't have a glass of milk in my hand and snacks in front of me, he's certain the baby will be undernourished. The man is driving me crazy.''

"Better you than me," Laurie murmured.

Patsy grinned. "I heard that. Has he been giving you a rough time?''

"No more than anyone else around here. I can't blame them, though. They just care about Harlan Patrick.''

"And about you and Amy Lynn," Patsy insisted. "That's the way this family is. They take everyone in if they know that a family member cares about them. They did with me.''

"But I'm not playing by the rules. I'm leaving again."

"Doesn't matter," Patsy insisted. "You're the mother of a great-grandbaby." She gave Laurie's hand a squeeze. "Around here that's all that counts."

"There you are," Justin said, walking toward them with a plate of appetizers in his hand. Pretty much ignoring Laurie, he shoved the plate under his wife's nose. "Try a little of this. It's your favorite cheese."

Patsy gave Laurie a weary grin. "See what I mean." She ignored the plate and started away from him. "Justin, I'm not hungry. I'm saving room for steak."

"One little bite," he encouraged, trailing after her.

Laurie's gaze followed them wistfully. She would have given anything to have had Harlan Patrick doting on her during her pregnancy.

But she had handled that time on her own, too. It had proved once and for all that she could cope with any curves life tossed her way, reassuring her that she would always be in control of her own destiny.

It was ironic, she supposed. She had proved to herself that she needed no one to survive, even to thrive, but rather than feeling triumphant, all she could think about these days was how very lonely she had been before Harlan Patrick had reappeared in that Montana nightclub.

Chapter Twelve

The barbecue was pure torment. Harlan Patrick retreated to the paddock with a cigarette he'd bummed
from Slade. To his surprise the hand had been
coaxed into joining the family—apparently by the
very woman he'd protested vehemently that he
wanted nowhere near him. Val had been looking
especially pleased with herself all evening. Harlan
Patrick was glad somebody's romance looked promising.

He hitched himself up on the split-rail fence and
tried not to light the cigarette or to think about Laurie. The last time he'd seen her she'd been telling
stories about the country music business and the
sometimes overzealous fans. She'd looked so alive,
almost as alive as she'd been in his arms down by
the creek that afternoon.

How could he even think about asking her to give up something that obviously brought her so much joy? How could he compete at all with the adulation of millions of fans? He was just one cowboy out of thousands who fantasized about her.

As he sat on the railing, he heard someone begin to strum a guitar. It might even have been his father, who professed to have musical talents, but sure as heck couldn't carry a tune. Harlan Patrick's heart clenched in anticipation. He knew it wouldn't take long once the music started for someone to coax Laurie into singing.

Sure enough, that low, sexy voice of hers caught on a breeze and carried to where he sat. It was a new song, one he hadn't heard before, and it was gut-wrenching, another surefire hit. Despite his instincts for self-preservation, he tossed aside the still unlit cigarette in disgust and began moving back toward the patio where everyone was gathered.

A security floodlight at the end of the patio bathed Laurie in a silvery glow as flattering as any spotlight. She had the guitar now, and her eyes were closed as she sang about lost love and past mistakes. Harlan Patrick had the feeling she was singing about the two of them, which made it all the harder to bear when the lovers in the song parted one last time.

As the last notes died, he was drawn to her side.

"That was beautiful," he said in a quiet voice not meant to be heard over the family's enthusiastic applause and catcalls. "A new song?"

Her gaze met his, and the rest of the crowd seemed to disappear.

"I've been working on it for a while now."

"That ending's a real tearjerker."

She shot him a knowing look. "It's the way it had to be."

His heart seemed to slow to a stop. "Then you don't see any way to change it?"

"Not offhand. Do you?"

He held out his hand. "Dance with me."

She glanced around. "There's no music."

"I can fix that. Come with me." When she hesitated, he grinned. "Dare you."

Her eyes sparkled with a hundred shared memories of the mischief those two words had gotten them into. After another moment's hesitation, she slipped her hand trustingly into his and went with him. He picked one of her CDs from a whole stack inside and slid it into the player, then turned the volume down low. This was for the two of them and no one else.

"We're not going back outside?" she asked.

"Scared to be alone with me, Laurie?"

"Of course not."

He tugged her gently into his arms. "Good. 'Cause I want you all to myself right now. Just you and me and this music that's so all-fired important to you."

She started to pull away, but he held her close. "That wasn't a put-down."

"It sounded like one."

"You know me, darlin'—sometimes I'm not as good with words as you are."

"Oh, please," she retorted impatiently. "Nobody

in Texas is better at a turn of phrase than you, Harlan Patrick. That's why women fall all over themselves chasing after you.''

"Maybe I should try my hand at writing songs, then," he suggested in jest.

She regarded him evenly, clearly taking the idea far more seriously than he'd intended. "Maybe you should."

"I'd be lousy at it."

"Why do you say that?"

"Because I'd be writing them with happy endings."

She sighed and rested her head against his chest. "You're right. You are the ultimate romantic."

He was amused by the wistful note in her voice. "Why is it that I have to fall for the only woman on earth who'd consider that a bad thing?"

"It's not a bad thing. It's just not very practical, especially in my line of work. Nothing sells better than a good ol' song about love gone wrong."

He pulled back and regarded her curiously. "Is that why you're so dead set on keeping us apart? Are you afraid if you and I have a happy ending, you'll lose your touch?"

She stared at him, clearly shocked by the suggestion. "Don't be ridiculous. I'm not turning myself inside out just so I can be inspired to write another song with a sad ending. People write about all sorts of things without having to live them. A decent mystery writer doesn't have to gun somebody down to write about it."

"You sound a little defensive. Are you so sure

you're not just the teensiest bit worried that loving me will ruin your way with a lovesick turn of phrase?'' he asked, because the more he thought about it, the more sense it made to him. ''You're afraid to be happy, Laurie. You think that well of misery that you draw on for your music will dry up if you're not careful.''

''That is the most absurd notion you've ever expressed, Harlan Patrick. I don't want to be miserable. I don't want to make you miserable.''

''Then do something to change it. Take a chance on us, Laurie. Come back here after your tour. If you won't marry me, live with me for a while. See what kind of balancing act we can come up with.''

''No,'' she said practically before the words were out of his mouth.

Pulse pounding with fury, he backed away from her. ''You didn't even think about it.''

''I don't have to think about it. I will not bring Amy Lynn to live here with you. It'll only confuse her when it's time for us to go.''

He slammed a fist into the wall, scraping his knuckles. ''Dammit, you won't even try, will you? I don't even matter that much to you.''

''You do matter,'' she insisted. ''But—''

''But what?''

''You'll overwhelm me, Harlan Patrick. If I do as you ask, it will be too easy to settle in and stay.''

''What the hell is wrong with that?''

''You know what's wrong with it,'' she insisted, tears streaming. ''I've told you. You just haven't been listening, as usual.''

"Because of your father?" he asked incredulously. "This is all because of a man who left you when you were four?"

"Yes," she said, regarding him defiantly. "Because the first man I loved, the one who was supposed to love me forever, walked out and there was nothing I could do to stop him."

He could hear the anguish in her voice and knew that her reasoning made perfect sense to her, even if it made next to none to him. He cupped her tear-streaked face in his hands.

"Sweetheart, I am nothing like your father. I'm not going to leave you. Not ever. We've been apart for years now, yet I'm still right here, waiting. Doesn't that prove anything at all to you?"

"That you're stubborn mostly," she said with a rueful expression. "You can't guarantee feelings. I could drive you away. I wouldn't mean to, but it could happen."

Finally he began to understand the real cause of her anguish. "Is that what you think happened with your dad? You think your mother did something to drive him away?"

"That must have been it."

He regarded her incredulously. "This is something that's so important to you that you're shutting me out because of it and you've never asked your mother what really happened?"

She shook her head. "I couldn't. I could see how she was hurting. She never mentioned him again, so neither did I."

"Then I think it's time you did."

"No. I can't."

"What are you really afraid of?" he asked, startled to think of the brave, adventurous woman who'd once taken any dare being scared of anything. He studied her intently, saw the shadows in her eyes and realized suddenly what it was. It was the nightmare of every child of divorced parents. Why hadn't he seen it sooner?

"You're afraid it was something you did that made him go, aren't you?" he asked quietly but insistently.

"Of course not. I was a kid, a baby, practically."

"That's right. You were a kid, and whatever happened was between grown-ups," he reminded her. "Laurie, you have to talk to your mom. Until you know for sure, until you lay that to rest, you will never let any man into your life. Do you want to spend the rest of your life alone?"

"I'm not alone," she said with a defiant thrust of her chin. "I have Amy Lynn and Val and the band. I'm surrounded by people."

"You can't make Amy Lynn your entire world," he argued. "It's too big a burden to put on a little girl. As for the others, there are no guarantees they'll stay, either."

"They will," she insisted.

Rather than arguing with her about the uncertainty of the future, he settled for forcing her to take a long hard look at the present. "Are they there when you get scared in the middle of the night? Can they keep you warm when it's cold? Can they kiss away your tears?"

He saw her struggling with the truth.

"No," she admitted finally, "but—"

"You deserve more, Laurie. You deserve someone who'll be there, someone who knows you inside and out, someone who's not just drawing a paycheck." He held up a hand before she could protest. "I know they care about you, but it's not the same." He gazed into her eyes. "Is it?"

She drew in a shuddering breath. "No," she conceded, her expression bleak. "It's not. But it's all I have."

"It doesn't have to be."

"Yes, it does," she insisted. "I can't risk any more."

He knew then that he was losing her all over again. "Talk to your mother," he pleaded again. "Please, Laurie. For us. For Amy Lynn. Find out what happened all those years ago."

Laurie was silent all the way back into town, struggling with herself. A part of her knew that Harlan Patrick was right. Her whole future, whether with him or someone else, rested on finding out the truth about what had happened all those years ago. She'd been hiding from the need to do it for years now, pretending that the long-ago hurt wasn't affecting every choice she made.

In fact, she had to wonder if her father wasn't the real reason she had remained so stubbornly determined to spend her life on the road, cramming in concert appearances in tiny, out-of-the-way places, hoping that one day she would glimpse a familiar face in the crowd. Even as the thought occurred to her, she knew that she had finally grasped something that had been eluding her for years.

"Oh, my God," she murmured.

Three startled faces turned to her in the car.

"What?" Harlan Patrick asked.

"Nothing," she said at once.

"Laurie, is everything okay?" her mother asked from the back seat.

She glanced over her shoulder and forced a smile for her mother and for an equally concerned Val. "Fine. I just remembered something, that's all."

Her gaze came to rest on her sleeping daughter, buckled securely into her car seat. Would Amy Lynn grow up with the same terrible insecurities if Laurie kept Harlan Patrick out of her life? Was she dooming her precious baby to the same sort of future she faced?

Never! She resolved then and there to begin looking for answers and she would start first thing in the morning, before she left for Ohio. As soon as she'd made the decision, she felt better, more at peace than she had in years. And she owed it to Harlan Patrick and his persistent refusal to take no for an answer. He had prodded her into heavy-duty soul-searching.

When they got to the house, she let the others go inside, lingering beside him in the car.

"Thank you," she said quietly.

"For what?"

"For forcing me to face the past."

"Have you really done that?"

She shrugged. "Not exactly, but I'm getting there.

I'm going to have that long-overdue talk with my mom in the morning. You could do me a huge favor if you'd come and take Amy Lynn and Val out for breakfast.''

"Gladly. I'll take 'em over to Dolan's. Sharon Lynn will love introducing another Adams to her cooking. The rest of us are proof that you can survive it.''

"You know perfectly well she makes the best hotcakes around.''

"When her mind's on it,'' he agreed with a grin. "Lately, with little Ashley getting ready for preschool, she's been listening to her biological clock ticking and she tends to get a little distracted. With Amy Lynn there for her to fuss over, I'm liable to have to do the cooking myself.''

"I'll warn Val,'' she promised.

He tucked a finger under her chin and turned her head to face him. "I'm glad you're going to do this.''

"I just pray I won't regret it.''

"You should never regret asking for the truth. It's living with lies and secrets and guesswork that'll do you in.''

"I suppose so.''

He leaned over and pressed a kiss against her forehead. "Sure you don't want me to be here when you talk to your mom?''

"No. I have to do this on my own.'' She rested her palm against his cheek. "Have I mentioned lately how much I love you?''

He smiled. "Every now and again, but I never

tire of hearing it. That's what keeps me hanging in here.''

"I wish things weren't so complicated.''

"Hey, darlin', what would be the challenge in that? Life's full of complications. Surviving them is what makes a person stronger.''

"Then I guess I've done my bit to see that you're as tough as Hercules.''

He winked at her. "Want to feel my muscles?''

"You wish. Don't start something you're not prepared to finish, cowboy.''

"Oh, I am always prepared when I'm around you.'' He brushed a kiss across her lips, then lingered.

Laurie felt the slow rise of heat in her blood, the tug of desire building low in her belly. It took so little for her to want him, so little to set her heart to racing. She backed away and drew in a deep breath.

"Hold that thought,'' she pleaded.

"Forever, if I have to.''

"Not that long,'' she promised, then slid out of the car. "I'll see you in the morning.''

"Bright and early,'' he agreed. "Sleep tight, darlin', and dream of me.''

He was already pulling away when she whispered, "I always do.''

Dreaming of Harlan Patrick was what would give her the courage to confront her mother in the morning. Imagining that confrontation was what kept her awake most of the night. She was already in the kitchen with the coffee going when Val wandered down at the crack of dawn.

"Coffee?" she murmured, yawning.

Laurie poured her a mug. "Would you do me a favor this morning?"

"Sure, anything."

"When Harlan Patrick comes by in a little while, will you take the baby and go out to breakfast with him? I need to have a talk with my mom."

"Of course," Val said, then studied her worriedly. "Is everything okay?"

"It will be," Laurie said grimly. "It has to be."

Val reached over and squeezed her hand. "I'll go get ready now. The baby should be awake, too. We'll be all set when Harlan Patrick gets here."

"Thanks. And thanks for not asking a lot of questions."

"You'll tell me what you can, when you can. Until then, I'll do whatever I can to help."

Alone again, Laurie sipped her second cup of coffee and tried to find the words she would need to ask her mother about what had happened all those years ago. She couldn't just blurt it out, not after all these years of polite silence. She had no idea what her mother's reaction would be. She'd been devastated back then, unable to hide the sorrow that had left deep shadows under her eyes and wiped the color from her cheeks.

Fortunately Harlan Patrick arrived and spirited Val and Amy Lynn away before her mother came downstairs.

"You here all alone?" she asked Laurie with evident surprise when she wandered into the kitchen just after eight. "I thought I heard Val and the baby stirring."

"Harlan Patrick took them to Dolan's to breakfast."

Her mother regarded her worriedly. "And you didn't want to go along? You and Harlan Patrick haven't fought again, have you?"

"No. I just wanted some time alone with you. Can I fix you something to eat?"

"Absolutely not. You stay where you are. I'll just have some cereal."

She poured cornflakes into a bowl as she had practically every day of her life that Laurie could remember. She added milk and sat down opposite Laurie. She stirred the cereal in the bowl, but didn't take a bite. Finally she lifted her gaze to clash with Laurie's.

"Okay, girl, what's on your mind? You didn't chase everybody out of here just so you and I could catch up, did you?"

"Not exactly."

"What then?"

Laurie drew in a deep breath. Feeling as if she were on the edge of a precipice, she finally forced herself to dive off. "I want to know about Dad."

The spoon slipped from her mother's grasp and clattered against the bowl. "Your father? Why on earth would you bring him up after all these years?"

"Because Harlan Patrick thinks he's the reason I won't make a commitment, and I've finally concluded he could be right."

"That's ridiculous. You barely even knew your father. He's been gone for more than twenty years now, and you've never asked about him once."

"That's why I'm asking now. I need to know everything, Mom. I need to know why he left. Was it something I did? Something you did? Have you ever heard from him again? Do you know where he is?"

"Well, I never…" Clearly agitated, her mother refused to meet her gaze.

Laurie reached across the table and clasped her mother's icy hand. "Please, Mom, it's important. Did I do something wrong? Is that why he left?"

"Don't be ridiculous. You were a child. He adored you."

"How can you say that? He walked away without ever looking back. He never sent so much as a card at Christmas or for my birthday."

Her comments were greeted with guilty silence. "Mom, he didn't, did he?" She stared at her mother in stunned horror. "He did send me something and you kept it from me. Why, Mom? Why would you do something like that?"

"You never asked about him," her mother retorted defensively. "I saw no need to go stirring things up."

"What did he send?"

With a look of utter defeat on her face, her mother stood up shakily and left the room. Laurie didn't try to stop her because something told her that at long last her mother wasn't running away from the past. She was going after it.

With her heart in her throat, Laurie waited. Her

mother came back into the room a few minutes later with a huge cardboard box in her arms.

"I should have thrown these away, I suppose," she murmured as she set the box in front of Laurie. "But I couldn't. I think I always knew this day would come."

Laurie stood and peered into the box that had been taped shut and labeled Old Bills, all but ensuring she would never open it. There were postcards and letters and greeting cards, all addressed in a firm, masculine handwriting. There were even a few small gifts, still wrapped in Christmas and birthday paper.

"Oh, sweet heaven," she murmured as tears filled her eyes and flowed down her cheeks.

"I'll leave you to go through this," her mother said.

"No," Laurie snapped. "Before you go, I want to know why. I want to know why he left."

"It was simple, really," her mother said wearily. "He didn't love me anymore."

"Falling out of love is never simple. Something must have happened. I heard you arguing that night. It must have been about something."

"Oh, baby, you have so much to learn about marriage. Even when both people love each other with all their hearts, it takes work and commitment to stay together, to have a relationship that grows stronger year after year. Your dad was tired of the struggle to make ends meet. He was tired of having to account for the money he spent or where he spent his time. He was tired of coming home to the same bed every night.''

''He had an affair?''

''No, not that I knew about, but he was bored with me, with marriage. And when he tired of it all, he left. My love wasn't enough to keep him here.''

She heard the raw pain in her mother's voice even after all these times and felt guilty for stirring it up again. ''Oh, Mom, I'm sorry.''

''Don't be. I accepted it long ago.''

''Did you really?'' Laurie wondered aloud. ''You kept all this from me.''

''Maybe I worried that if you knew he wanted to see you, you would choose him over me. I hope that's not why, but it might have been. I told myself I was doing what was best for you, keeping you with somebody who would always love you, who wouldn't turn away no matter what.'' She regarded Laurie sadly. ''Was I so very wrong to do that?''

''I should have had a choice,'' Laurie whispered. ''It was my choice to make.''

''You were four years old,'' her mother retorted sharply.

''If not then, later. When I was eight or ten or even seventeen.''

''By then it was too late.''

Laurie's heart thudded dully. ''He's dead?''

''No, I just lost track of him. The cards and packages stopped when you were barely ten. I guess he gave up.''

Laurie vowed then and there to find him. If he was still alive, she would find her father again and get his side of the story. Maybe even after all this time, they could try to build some sort of relationship with each other. Maybe he would be someone she would want in her life. Maybe he wouldn't be, but this time she would have the chance to choose.

And then, at last, maybe she would find the peace that had eluded her for so many years.

Chapter Thirteen

When Harlan Patrick walked back into the Jensen kitchen two hours later, he found Laurie still seated at the kitchen table, surrounded by papers. Her face was streaked with tears, her eyes puffy. She was holding an unopened package, its bright red Santa wrapping paper incongruous on the hot summer day.

"I can't open it," she told him quietly, not looking up. "I can't take my eyes off of it, but I can't open it."

He guessed at once who had sent the gift, and how very long ago. "It's from your father."

She nodded. "My mother saved it." She gestured toward the postcards and birthday cards littering the table. "All of this, and I never knew."

"He must have missed you very much."

"He said he did," she said in a soft, disbelieving voice. She set the package on the table and reached for a postcard. "See here, he says he loves me, that he wishes I were with him."

Harlan Patrick noted that the card was from Dallas. Laurie chose another one, from California.

"He said it here, too," she told him. "He was at the beach." She met Harlan Patrick's gaze with tear-swollen eyes. "Did you know I'd never been to the beach, not until my first concert stop in Los Angeles? That was the first time I saw the ocean. He could have been right there, and I would never have known it."

"Are other things postmarked from Los Angeles?"

Startled, she stared at him. "I don't know. I only read the messages."

He held out his hand. "Let me see." He watched her closely. "That is if you're interested in finding him."

"You know I am," she said vehemently. "I have to."

"Then I'll help."

Her eyes brightened for the first time. "You will?"

"Of course I will. We'll find him together, Laurie. That's a promise."

"And you always keep your promises."

"If I can."

"No," she said, suddenly angry. "Always, Harlan Patrick. You have to say it."

Startled by her burst of fury, he could only guess

at the cause. "Your mom's been telling you that promises don't mean much, hasn't she?"

She sighed wearily. "Pretty much."

"Mine do." He glanced at the package on the table. "Why don't you open that now, darlin'?"

"No," she said, tucking the tiny package into her pocket. "I think I'll save it and open it when we find him."

Harlan Patrick knew then that his whole future rested on finding Laurie's father and putting the past to rest once and for all. The sooner he could make that happen, the better. Fortunately he had a cousin who was a sheriff. Justin ought to be able to get the ball rolling before the day was out.

But if Justin ran into a dead end, there were private investigators. Hell, he'd go chasing after the man himself, if that's what it took.

Anxious to get started, he stood up and dropped a quick kiss on Laurie's forehead. "You get your things together, sweetheart. We'll take off for Ohio in a couple of hours. Meantime I have some things I need to do."

"What things?"

"Odds and ends," he said evasively, refusing to get her hopes up until he'd had a talk with Justin about just how difficult this search was likely to be. "Be ready when I get back, okay?"

"Sure," she said distractedly, already lost in another of her father's letters.

"Maybe I'll turn the packing over to Val," he murmured as he left the room. Laurie's mind clearly wasn't likely to be on anything except her daddy for some time to come.

A few minutes later he sat in Justin's office and pleaded his case.

"You want me to track down Laurie's father?" Justin repeated.

"As a favor to me. She needs to put an end to all the wondering."

"Any idea where I might start this search?"

"California. The last cards and letters he sent came from a little town just north of Los Angeles."

"And when was that?"

"About ten, maybe fifteen years ago, judging by the postmarks. I don't think there was anything more recent than that. I suppose he just gave up when he never heard back from her."

"Do you honestly think he's been staying put all this time?"

"Maybe not, but it's a starting point. Surely a bright law-enforcement officer such as yourself can be clever enough to follow his trail after that."

"Flattery won't help."

"Bribery, then? Blackmail?"

Justin regarded him with indignation. "You'd resort to that, wouldn't you?"

Harlan Patrick grinned. "Oh, yeah, and who knows all your sins better than me?"

Justin didn't flinch at the threat. In fact, he seemed to be considering it thoughtfully. "Okay, then. Let's concentrate on the bribery for a second."

His straight-arrow cousin was open to bribery, actually soliciting it? Harlan Patrick couldn't wait to hear what he had in mind. "Okay. What'll it take?"

"Patsy and I want to build a new house on that land granddaddy intends to leave me out at White Pines."

Harlan Patrick's gaze narrowed. He wasn't sure he liked where this was heading. Justin had always been very sneaky about tricking him into hard work, then taking off for parts unknown. "Exactly what does that have to do with me?" he asked suspiciously.

"We need labor. We need a strong back and lots of sweat. We want to do this ourselves."

"Excuse me, but I see a slight contradiction here. If you want to build this all by your little lonesomes, why am I involved?"

"Because Patsy's pregnant, in case you haven't noticed. She might be able to hold a hammer, but it's doubtful she could get close enough to actually hit a nail."

"You'd better not let her hear you say that," Harlan Patrick warned. "I'm told women are very sensitive on the subject of their waistlines, especially this late in a pregnancy. Besides, she won't be pregnant forever. Isn't the baby due any minute now?"

"True, but I'd like to have the frame of the house up as a surprise on the day we bring the baby home from the hospital."

"Maybe you ought to go for walls, too, or were you intending to sell her on the idea of open-air living?"

"Very funny. I'm not planning on making her

live there yet. I just want to show her it's under way. Can I count on you?''

In exchange for a future with Laurie? He didn't even hesitate. ''I'll give you twenty-four hours a day as soon as I get Laurie up to Ohio.'' He regarded Justin evenly. ''What about you, then? Can I count on you?''

Justin grinned. ''Was there ever any doubt? I'm a cop. Nobody loves a good mystery more than me.''

''Thanks. I owe you.''

''Oh, yeah, and I intend to start collecting first thing tomorrow.''

''Tomorrow? I was thinking of spending one day in Ohio before I came back.''

''Tomorrow,'' Justin repeated. ''I can't count on this baby waiting around much longer. Patsy looks as if she's about to pop.''

''I'll be back tonight,'' Harlan Patrick agreed with regret. He'd hoped for a long night with Laurie back in his arms. Maybe this was just as well, though. When they were together the next time, he wanted her full attention and he seriously doubted he would have it until she'd finally found her daddy.

Laurie was startled when they got to her hotel in Columbus and Harlan Patrick stayed outside the room, rather than following her inside. She'd also been a bit bemused by his lack of persistence when it came to keeping Amy Lynn with him for the next couple of weeks, but she'd been so grateful that she hadn't questioned that.

"You're not coming in?"

He shook his head. "I've got to get right back to Texas."

"But I thought—"

"I'll be back before you know it, darlin'."

Conflicting emotions tore through her. She'd expected him to stay, to plague her about coming home, to be in her face for the next two weeks. It should have been a relief to know that he was leaving. It wasn't. He was standing right next to her, and already she felt alone and abandoned.

"Why?" she asked, because she'd never gotten a chance to ask another man that very question. "Why are you leaving?"

"You're going to be very busy the next couple of weeks, and I have some things to do. You won't even have time to miss me."

She missed him already.

He tilted her chin up. "I will be back. I promised Justin I'd help him with something, a surprise for Patsy. It'll take a few days, maybe a week or two."

"Fine. You do what you have to do," she said finally, ungraciously.

He chuckled. "A man could almost get the idea that you're not anxious to see me leave."

She drew herself up and resorted to her haughtiest demeanor. "Don't be silly. I never wanted you trailing after me in the first place."

"When did you change your mind?" he asked, bending closer. "Was it when I did this?"

His mouth settled over hers, and his tongue slid

between her lips. Laurie eased into the kiss as naturally as breathing.

"Or this?" he inquired, his hand doing a slow sweep over her hip before finally coming to rest just below her breast.

Her pulse raced.

He leaned back and gazed into her eyes. His own eyes were the deep, mysterious blue of dawn with the promise of excitement to come. His hand closed over her breast, and his thumb scraped over the nipple until she gasped with the wicked sweetness of the sensation.

"Could it be that?' he asked, laughter in his eyes now.

"If you have any other alternatives you intend to demonstrate, perhaps we ought to take this inside," she suggested breathlessly.

"Oh, you'd like that, wouldn't you?" he taunted. "Knowing that you could keep me here and have your way with me?"

Laurie felt a grin spreading across her face. "You bet." Her smile broadened. "Dare you."

Before she realized what he intended, he scooped her into his arms, walked into the room and kicked the door shut behind them.

"Darlin', don't you know better than to dare a man like me?"

She chuckled at his predictability and at the fire that made his skin burn to her touch. "Got you," she taunted.

"Oh, no," he said, heading for the suite's bedroom. "I've got you."

And in case she had any doubts about that, he spent the next several hours proving it.

It was dawn before he left, sneaking from the bed that smelled of perfume and sex. He bent over to drop a kiss against her cheek.

"I'll be back before you know it," he promised. "Unless Justin murders me for being late this morning."

"Love you," she told him with a yawn.

"Remember that when you wake up," he teased, and then he was gone.

Laurie's eyes flew open at the sound of the door clicking softly closed. "I'll never forget it again," she whispered. "Never."

Just as he had predicted, that day and the next she was so busy that she hardly had a second to spare. Val had lined up newspaper and television interviews, along with drop-in visits to a couple of country-music radio stations. At night there were her appearances at the Ohio State Fair, where the temperatures were wickedly hot, the air still and muggy. The wildly enthusiastic crowds more than made up for the discomfort.

It was only late at night that Laurie realized that she hadn't heard a word from Harlan Patrick, but by then it was too late to call and morning brought a new and demanding round of commitments.

From Columbus the tour moved on to Cleveland, then west to Indianapolis, then south to Louisville. She was getting closer to home again, but for some reason she didn't care to explore too closely the allure of Nashville wasn't what it once had been. Something inside her knew that that brief visit to Los Piños had reminded her that her real home was in Texas and always would be.

Back in her dressing room after another wildly successful concert, she sorted through the stack of messages Val had left for her, hoping for one from Harlan Patrick. Nothing. She told herself she wasn't disappointed, but the truth was that she felt let down and scared. It was as if he, too, had vanished from her life.

Val wandered into the dressing room carrying Amy Lynn.

"I thought you were taking her to the hotel," Laurie said, reaching for her wide-awake daughter.

"Your daughter woke up about an hour ago and started fussing. Nothing I could do seemed to settle her down, so I figured we'd come on over here and see if seeing her mama could help."

Laurie looked into those wide blue eyes, shimmering with unshed tears, and thought of other blue eyes she'd like to be staring into about now. How had she gone for so long without Harlan Patrick around? Could she ever do it again? She took the baby from Val.

"What's wrong, darling girl? Are you missing your daddy?"

Amy Lynn stared back at her. "Da?" she said wistfully.

Laurie grinned. "Val, did you hear that? She said her first word. She said, 'Da.'"

"Are you going to call Harlan Patrick and tell him that?"

"I can't. It's nearly midnight. He's probably been asleep for hours. Ranchers get up at the crack of dawn."

Val grinned. "Something tells me he wouldn't mind losing a little sleep for this news. Besides, you've been missing him like crazy. Call. Maybe then both you and the little one here would actually get a good night's rest."

Laurie thought it over, then nodded. "You're right." She reached for the phone and punched in Harlan Patrick's number. It seemed like an eternity before he answered, his voice thick with sleep.

"Yeah, what?"

Laurie held the phone up to Amy Lynn's mouth. "Say it," she whispered. "It's your daddy."

Amy Lynn studied the phone quizzically, then said loudly, "Da?"

Laurie heard Harlan Patrick's hoot even before she put the receiver back to her own ear. "You heard?"

"She said 'Daddy,' didn't she?"

"Close enough," Laurie agreed. "Isn't she the most brilliant child on the face of the earth?"

"Absolutely. Just one question, though. What's she doing up at this hour?"

"She was missing you." Her voice dropped a notch. "So was I."

"The same goes for me."

"You haven't called."

"That's because I'm working for a slave driver.

Once Justin gets a notion in his head, he pulls out all the stops.''

"Exactly what are the two of you up to?"

"Justin's not up to much, if you ask me. I'm doing all the physical labor. He seems to have designated himself as supervisor. The man has no shame at all. He's blatantly using me."

"And what does he have you doing?"

"Building a house for him and Patsy out here at White Pines. It won't even be close to finished before the baby's born, but he wants to surprise her with the frame at least."

"I had no idea you knew how to build a house."

"Actually I'm not so sure I'd want to live in any house I built, but I can swing a hammer and follow directions. Besides, it was a fair trade for what I want from Justin."

"Which is?"

"He's doing a little research for me."

Laurie's heart climbed into her throat. "He's looking for my father, isn't he?"

"He's trying," Harlan Patrick admitted slowly. "Don't get your hopes up, though. So far, all he's run into are dead ends."

"At least he's trying," she whispered. "Thank you."

"I told you I'd do what I could. Now tell me about the tour. Is it going well? I saw the piece on TV the other night. Mom called me when she heard the promotion for it. I think that show's ratings probably went through the roof here in Los Piños. Grandpa Harlan called right afterward. Then Sharon

Lynn called. The consensus was that you looked beautiful and sounded brilliant.''

She laughed. "You all aren't biased, by any chance?''

"Maybe just a little," he agreed, then yawned. "Sorry."

"No, it's late and I'd better let you go. I just wanted you to know that your daughter and I were thinking about you."

"Are you at the hotel?"

"No, we're still in my dressing room. I'm heading back there now."

"Sleep well, darlin'."

"You, too. I miss you."

"Not half as much as I miss you. Give my girl a kiss for me."

"You want to tell her good-night?"

"Absolutely."

Laurie took Amy Lynn back from Val and held the phone to her ear. "Here she is," she told Harlan Patrick.

She could hear the low hum of his voice as he talked to Amy Lynn, saw her puzzled frown and then a gurgle of delight as she realized once again that it was her daddy.

"Da," she repeated joyously, patting the phone. "Da!"

When Laurie tried to take the phone away, Amy Lynn's face screwed up. "Da," she echoed piteously.

"Tell him bye-bye," Laurie coached.

Amy Lynn waved instead.

"She's waving," Laurie told him.

"I don't want to miss any more firsts," Harlan Patrick said. "I want to be there."

Laurie sighed. She understood his longing. "I know."

"I'll see you both soon," he promised.

"Good night, Harlan Patrick."

"Night, darlin'."

Neither of them seemed to have the will to sever the connection. Finally, with a sigh, Laurie placed the receiver back on the hook.

"Feel better?" Val asked.

"No."

"Hearing his voice doesn't do it for you?"

"It only made me miss him more." She regarded her assistant and admitted the painful truth. "This is why it won't work, you know. It hurts too much to be apart. We'll just end up making each other miserable."

"Did it hurt any less when you thought you'd never see him again?"

Startled by the question, Laurie paused thoughtfully. "No," she conceded finally.

"Then isn't it better to know that you will be together again, that this misery is just temporary?"

"You're right," she said, excited by the discovery. "I hadn't looked at it that way." She gave her assistant a hug. "Thank you."

"That's why you pay me the big bucks," Val said.

"Do I pay you big bucks?"

"Not big enough," Val retorted, then added with confidence, "But you will."

"Yes, I imagine I will," Laurie agreed. "And whenever I start wallowing in self-pity, remind me again of the alternative."

"It's a deal."

"How many more days on this tour?"

"Seven more days, six more concerts, then back to Nashville."

"Back to Texas," Laurie corrected.

"But—"

"Make it happen, Val. Whatever you have to do."

Val grinned. "In return for those big bucks you're going to start paying me, consider it as good as done."

Chapter Fourteen

Three days after that middle-of-the-night call from
Laurie, Harlan Patrick was hammering the last nail
home in the frame for Justin's new house when his
cousin drove up.

"Excellent timing," he called down to him from
his perch on the skeletal rooftop. "Have you actually put up one board in this place?"

Justin shifted his Stetson back on his head and
stared up through reflective sunglasses. "No need.
You're doing just fine."

"What brings you by, since it's obviously not to
help out?"

"I found Buzz Jensen."

Harlan Patrick felt his heart begin to thud.
"Alive?"

"Oh, yeah."

He didn't like the sound of that.

"I'll be right down."

He climbed down the ladder braced against what would eventually be the kitchen wall and headed for a cooler he'd filled with ice and soft drinks. Regretting that it wasn't a beer, he popped the top on one can, took a long swallow, then met his cousin's gaze.

"Okay, give it to me. Is he in jail or something?"

"No, but he is married again."

Harlan Patrick took that news in stride. "I suppose that's to be expected. He left Laurie's mom a long time ago."

Justin stirred uncomfortably. "But the way I understand it, he never divorced her because she didn't believe in divorce."

"You're kidding me, right?"

"No. I checked it out myself. Mary Jensen told me she'd refused to give him a divorce."

"That means the man's a bigamist," Harlan Patrick said.

"With a happy new family in California, none of whom apparently have a clue about his past in Texas," Justin confirmed. "Unless he found some way around the legal system that I can't figure out."

"Well, hell," Harlan Patrick muttered. "This is a wrinkle I hadn't counted on. What am I supposed to do now?"

"I don't see that you have any choice. You promised Laurie you'd find her father for her. You've done that and you're going to have to tell her."

"How's she going to take it when she finds out he's got this whole new family? Hell's bells, how are they going to take it when they discover that he's been living a lie? What kind of can of worms are we opening here?"

"That's the trouble with searching for the truth," Justin noted. "Sometimes you find out a whole lot more than you ever wanted to know."

"Maybe you're wrong," Harlan Patrick said. "Maybe Buzz Jensen did get a divorce."

"Without Mary knowing about it?"

"It's possible," Harlan Patrick persisted.

"Doubtful," his cousin countered. He removed his sunglasses and met Harlan Patrick's gaze. "What are you going to do?"

"What do you think? I'm going to California."

"With Laurie?"

"Not on your life. I'm going on my own to check things out first. I'm not taking her there until we know the whole story."

"And then?"

He raked a hand through his hair. "I wish to hell I knew."

Five hours later, just past dinnertime, he was driving up to a small ranch-style house on a hillside just north of Los Angeles. The lawn was well tended, window boxes were filled with brightly colored flowers and toys and bicycles were scattered across the yard. A sedan that needed a paint job and a newer pickup sat in the driveway. Evidence of normal, everyday people just trying to get by, he concluded.

With a sigh of regret, Harlan Patrick climbed out of his car and walked toward the house. If this hadn't been the only way to get the answers Laurie needed, he wasn't sure he could have brought himself into these people's lives to tear apart their tidy little world.

When he rang the bell, the door was answered by a teenage girl who bore such a striking resemblance to Laurie that it almost took his breath away. He'd always assumed Laurie had inherited her looks from her mother, but it was clear now that she had a good bit of her father in her, too.

"Hi," she said with the same flirtatious, infectious grin that Laurie had used to captivate him years earlier. "Who're you?"

"Harlan Patrick Adams."

"Well, hey, Harlan Patrick. I'm Tess. What can I do for you?"

He had to hide a grin at the blatant suggestiveness she managed to put into those few little words. "I'd like to see your father if he's at home."

"Sure," she said at once. "Would you like to come in?"

Her open, trusting nature made him feel like a heel. This was going to be tough enough without going inside. "No, thanks," he said with a smile. "I'll wait right here."

"Hey, Dad," she bellowed. "Somebody here to see you." She regarded Harlan Patrick with interest as they waited. "I could get you something to drink if you like. Maybe a soda?"

"Nothing, thanks."

A middle-aged man came from the back of the house. He gave the girl a stern look. "How many times have I asked you not to shout all the way through the house? You could have come and told me we had company."

"I didn't want to leave him standing on the doorstep all by himself," she said. She gave Harlan Patrick a last wistful look. "See you."

"Bye. Thanks for your help."

After she'd gone, Buzz Jensen faced him. "What can I do for you?"

"I'm Harlan Patrick Adams," he said quietly. "From Los Piños."

As he mentioned the name of the town, he saw the man's shoulders sag with defeat. Dread spread across his face. He came out onto the front stoop and closed the door behind him.

"Why are you here? What do you want?"

"Just to talk, if you don't mind."

"Is it Mary? Has something happened to her?" There was genuine concern in his tone, that and a hint of panic.

"No. It's about Laurie."

The man staggered visibly. "Nothing's happened to her, has it? I would have heard. It would have been on TV."

Worried by the man's sudden pallor, Harlan Patrick took his arm and guided him to a lawn chair. "Are you okay?"

"Just surprised, that's all. Tell me what's happened."

"Laurie's fine."

He shook his head as if to clear it. "Then why are you here?"

"She's been asking a lot of questions lately. She's been thinking about you, wondering why you left all those years ago." Harlan Patrick looked the older man straight in the eye. "I love her, sir, but, you see, she's afraid I'll leave her the way you did. She needs to understand what happened back then before she can trust me or any other man."

"Hasn't she asked her mother?"

"She has, but it's not enough. There's a bond between a father and daughter. I'm only beginning to realize it myself." He met the older man's gaze evenly. "You see, Laurie and I have a baby girl."

He seemed startled by that. "You're the one, then. I saw that tabloid picture of her and the baby. I wondered who was responsible for getting her into trouble."

"I never knew about the baby, not until that picture. You have to believe that. There is no way I wouldn't have been there for her if I'd known."

Buzz Jensen nodded in sudden understanding. "You're one of those Adamses, aren't you? I should have guessed it straight off. Named after your grand-daddy. Honor's a big thing with an Adams."

"Yes, sir. So is family."

"Is that why you're here, instead of Laurie. You want to buy me off or something?"

"No. I wanted to see you, talk to you, make sure that arranging for Laurie to see you wouldn't lead to more hurt for her."

"I would never hurt her," he said indignantly.

"You already have," Harlan Patrick reminded him quietly. "That's the problem."

Buzz Jensen uttered a sigh of acknowledgment. "I suppose you're right."

"What about your family? Do they know about Laurie? Will they be hurt by all of this when the whole story comes out?"

"My wife knows," he acknowledged.

Harlan Patrick hesitated, then forced himself to ask, "Does she know you never divorced Laurie's mother?"

He nodded. "She accepted that we couldn't be married."

Harlan Patrick was relieved to know the man wasn't a bigamist, after all. That didn't make the situation a whole lot less complicated, though. "What about your kids?"

"They don't know about it." His expression turned defiant. "I don't want them to."

"I don't see how you can avoid it," Harlan Patrick countered. "Not if you see Laurie. They'll have questions."

"You can't bring her here," he said adamantly. "It's as simple as that."

Harlan Patrick was shocked by the decision. "You won't see her? Not even after what I've told you? How can you do that to her?"

"I didn't say I wouldn't see her. I said she couldn't come here. If you want to set up a meeting for somewhere else, I'll go." His eyes filled with tears. "I never thought I'd have the chance to see my baby girl again. I thought I'd go to my grave knowing that I'd failed her and that she'd never forgiven me.''

There was so much pain and sincerity in his voice that Harlan Patrick had no choice but to believe him. ''She never knew about the cards and letters,'' he told him then. ''Her mother kept them from her until recently.''

Buzz Jensen's hands shook as he reached over to clasp Harlan Patrick's hand and relief washed over his face. ''Thank you for telling me that. You don't know how hard I prayed that it was something like that. I didn't want to believe she'd just forgotten all about me.''

''No, sir, Laurie never forgot.'' He stared straight into the older man's eyes. ''But the time has come to help her let go.''

''Just tell me what you want me to do.''

''If you can leave first thing in the morning, I'll take you to her.''

He nodded. ''I'll make the arrangements.''

''Seven o'clock, then. I'll pick you up.''

''I'll be waiting,'' Buzz Jensen promised, his expression eager despite the questions the people inside were likely to have about the stranger who'd come calling.

Later, alone in a nearby motel, Harlan Patrick thought back over the meeting and tried to reassure himself that it was all going to work out. Or was he just setting a whole lot of people up for heartache?

As she left the stage after the last Louisville concert, Laurie was totally, thoroughly drained. All she wanted was to take a long hot shower and crawl into bed. Before she could do that, though, she had a group of VIP fans waiting to meet her backstage.

Val arranged these meet-and-greet sessions at the behest of local radio stations. When she wasn't so tired, Laurie actually enjoyed them. Tonight, though, she could barely keep her eyes open. An idea for a new song had come to her the night before right at bedtime, and she'd stayed awake most of the night fiddling with it. A half-hour nap before tonight's show hadn't made up for the lost sleep.

As she walked into the green room where drinks and hors d'oeuvres had been set up, she forced a smile and moved from one cluster of people to another, making small talk, thanking the DJs who played her music, flattering their wives and sponsors. For a solid hour she played the part of gracious hostess, before Val whipped in and whispered in her ear.

"What?" she asked, staring at her assistant incredulously.

"Harlan Patrick's here," Val repeated. "He's in your dressing room."

"Why didn't you bring him in here?"

"He wanted to wait there," Val said. "I'll make your excuses. Go."

Laurie didn't have to be urged twice. She flew down the hall and threw open the dressing-room door, but instead of Harlan Patrick, there was a stranger waiting, an older man who looked vaguely, disturbingly familiar. Her breath lodged in her throat.

The man stood slowly, took a hesitant step toward her, then stopped. "Hi, baby."

"Oh, my God," she murmured, thunderstruck. "It's you."

"It's your daddy," he confirmed.

Filled with wonder, she stepped closer, reached up with trembling fingers and touched his lined cheek, traced the deeper grooves that fanned out from the corners of his eyes—lines that hadn't been there the last time she'd seen him.

But the scent of his aftershave was the same, tantalizing her with the memory of being lifted high in strong arms, then cuddled against a broad chest.

"It really is you," she said in amazement. "But how did you get here?"

"Harlan Patrick found me. He came to California and brought me here."

She realized then that he was in the room, too, standing to the side, watching intently as if ready to intercede the instant the meeting started to sour. She rushed into his arms.

"Thank you," she said, peppering his face with kisses. "Thank you."

"You're okay?" he asked, searching her face.

"Better than okay," she said, tears flowing freely down her cheeks.

"Why don't we get out of here, then?" he suggested. "You two could use someplace private to get reacquainted. I've already talked to the sitter about staying with Amy Lynn till I get there."

"Yes, of course. The hotel, then." She gazed at

her father. "I'll get you a room, next to mine if possible."

"Already done," Harlan Patrick said.

"He doesn't miss much, this fellow of yours," her father said with evident admiration.

"No," she agreed. "He doesn't miss much."

At the hotel Harlan Patrick retreated to the adjoining suite while she and her father sat opposite each other. Suddenly she was as tongue-tied as a four-year-old confronted with a stranger.

"I don't know what to say to you, what to ask," she admitted eventually.

"Would it help if I told you I was pretty much at a loss, too?"

"Some," she said with a smile that came and went. Finally she blurted out the only question that really mattered, the one that had tormented her for all these years. "Why, Daddy? Why did you go?"

"What has your mother told you?"

"Just that you were bored, that you needed to move on."

He regarded her with regret. "Sad to say, that's probably as close to the truth as I could tell you. I was immature and irresponsible back then. I wasn't ready to be tied down. I tried—for five years I did the best I could—and then I just had to go."

The glib explanation filled her with anger. "You make it sound so simple, as if you were walking away from a business deal that wasn't to your advantage. Didn't I matter to you at all?"

He seemed stung by the accusation. "Of course you did. I regretted leaving you more than anything, but I couldn't see any other way to figure out what kind of man I was. I suppose I thought I'd come back one day or that you'd come and visit me, but then this and that happened and I just stayed away, built a new life. When I never heard a word from either of you, I figured you and your mama had done the same.''

''I just found out about the postcards, the letters, everything you sent back then.''

''That's what Harlan Patrick told me. I'm sorry, baby. I didn't know your mother would keep them from you. After a while, when I knew you were old enough to answer and you didn't, I figured it didn't matter to you anymore.''

''You were my father,'' she said angrily. ''How could you not matter to me?''

''I'd been gone a long time.''

''But you were my father,'' she repeated.

''I'm sorry, baby.''

He opened his arms and after a long hesitation, Laurie moved into them. ''But I'm back in your life now and this time I'll be a part of it for as much or as little as you want.''

''Are you still in California?''

He hesitated, then nodded. ''Yes.''

''I'll come to visit,'' she said at once. ''And bring Amy Lynn. Wait until you see her. She's beautiful.''

''I saw the picture in the tabloid. I couldn't believe I was really a granddaddy.'' He met her gaze, then glanced away, his expression guilty. ''You can't come there, Laurie. Much as I want you to, you can't.''

Her whole body seemed to go cold at his words. "Why?"

"Because I have a new family now, a boy and a girl. They…" He looked as if he might weep. "They don't know about you."

She stared at him in shock. "But you and Mama—"

"That's right. We never divorced, so you see why I can't let you come. They're too young to understand what I've done to them. Their mother knows, but we've protected the kids. My girl's a teenager. She's at that impressionable age when this could tear her world apart."

"You have another daughter," she repeated, her voice flat as she envisioned a girl who'd grown up with her father's love and attention the way she should have, the way she'd never had a chance to.

"How could you?" she asked, her emotions raging. "How could you do that to them? To me? What kind of man would do that?"

"One who's weak," he said at once. "A strong man would have stayed in Texas, made his marriage work, but I wasn't strong then and I wasn't strong when I settled down with Lucille in California, but she knew the truth. That's how I justified it."

"There is no justification," Laurie all but shouted as she saw her happy ending slipping away.

He sighed deeply. "You're right. There is no justification."

"So this is it, then? You drop in, say hi and then run back to the life you've built on a lie? I'm supposed to wait around for you to sneak away for an occasional visit with me, an unfortunate reminder of the past you left behind.'' She stood up and glowered down at him. ''Well, thanks, but no thanks. As of this moment, I no longer have a father. I no longer need one in my life.''

She reached for her purse, fumbled inside until she found the package she'd been carrying with her ever since its discovery. She took one last look at the bright paper, then flung it in her father's face. ''Give this to your other daughter, the one who matters.''

''Laurie,'' he whispered, reaching for her.

''No,'' she said furiously, backing away and opening the door. She took one last look at her father's haggard face, his shattered expression, and then she walked out and quietly closed the door behind her.

When she walked into the room next door, Harlan Patrick was waiting. He looked up at her entrance, studied her face, then opened his arms. She ran into them and burst into tears.

''He still won't let me be a part of his life,'' she whispered brokenly. ''He still doesn't want me.''

''You know that's not true,'' he consoled her. ''It's complicated. There are other people to consider. Maybe one day he'll find a way to tell them everything. In the meantime can't you accept that he does love you? He dropped everything and came here the minute I contacted him. Isn't that proof of how he feels?''

She wished it were, but it wasn't. Not when the bottom line was that he would be walking out again and leaving her behind.

Chapter Fifteen

Laurie was inconsolable. By morning she had retreated into a bleak silence that tore Harlan Patrick's soul in two. No matter what he said to her, no matter how he pleaded with her to make allowances for her father's new circumstances, she saw only that she was being essentially abandoned all over again.

"But I'm not leaving," he reminded her. "I'm right here."

"I know," she said quietly. "And I'm grateful. I really am."

"I don't want your gratitude, Laurie. I love you. This is where I want to be."

"No," she said with a shake of her head, her expression sad. "You want to be back in Texas, where you belong."

Harlan Patrick sighed. "Okay, yes, I want to be at White Pines, but I want you and Amy Lynn with me. You're the two people I love most in this world."

But no matter what he said, it wasn't enough. She had convinced herself that her father's decision to keep her and his new family apart meant she was somehow unworthy of his love, that no man would ever be able to love her.

"Dammit, Laurie, can't you see that he's the one who's losing here? This is costing him the love of a woman who's beautiful, talented, generous and kindhearted. Blame him. Hell, hate him if you want, but don't turn this back on yourself. Don't start thinking that you're the one who's unlovable again. I'm here to tell you it's not true. Doesn't my opinion count for anything?"

She regarded him with eyes dulled by hurt. "Of course, but—"

"But I'm not your father," he supplied, defeated.

"I'm sorry."

"You don't have to be sorry, dammit!" He raked his hand through his hair and tried to think of some way to get through to her, some way to bring back her spirit. She should have been spitting mad now, not resigned, but nothing he could think of to say or do even touched her.

Two days later he was at his wit's end. So was everyone else around her. She'd insisted Val cancel half a dozen interviews. Her concert performances had been lackluster, the reviews damning. She was dying inside and killing her career in the process.

Watching her do it to herself was excruciating for Harlan Patrick.

"You have to do something," Val said, blasting into Laurie's hotel suite with a handful of clippings in her hand. "I just got off the phone with Nick. He's getting rumblings about promoters wanting to back out of concert dates scheduled for the fall. She's destroying herself."

"I know," he said quietly. "I can see it, but I have no idea what to do. I can't get through to her. Other than when she's with Amy Lynn, it's as if she's just going through the motions of living."

"I'm scared for her," Val said. "I've never seen her like this before, not even when she found out she was pregnant and refused to tell you about it. I know she felt very much alone then, but expecting your baby gave her a reason to keep going. Her whole focus was on Amy Lynn and her music. Now she's about to lose her music, and it doesn't even seem to matter to her."

Harlan Patrick heard every word Val said, and an idea began to take shape in his mind. It was drastic and very, very risky. Laurie might never forgive him for it. In the end he could lose her; he could lose everything.

But if it worked, if it got her attention and made her start to live again, it would be worth it, he concluded.

"I know what I have to do," he said finally.

"What?"

"Just leave it to me. It'll be better if you don't know ahead of time." He clasped Val's shoulders and leveled a look into her eyes. "Just remember that I am doing this for Laurie, not to hurt her, okay? Remember that."

"Harlan Patrick," she began worriedly.

"It'll be fine," he reassured her as he grabbed his bag and packed his belongings.

"You're leaving?" she asked, clearly shocked.

He nodded. "I'm going back to Texas. Tell Laurie that and tell her she'll be hearing from me any day now. Tell her I've had enough."

"Enough?" she echoed. "What does that mean? Harlan Patrick, what are you planning?"

He dropped a kiss on her cheek. "Keep an eye on her for me. She's going to need you."

"Oh, my God," she whispered as he reached the door. "You're going to file for custody of Amy Lynn, aren't you? Aren't you?"

He nodded.

"Are you sure about this?"

"I can't think of any other way to make her fight, can you?"

"No, but what if she doesn't? What if she's not strong enough to fight you?"

Harlan Patrick refused to consider that. He knew that she would never let her daughter go, would never let Amy Lynn feel the pain of abandonment Laurie had felt her whole life long.

"Oh, she'll fight," he said with confidence. "I'm anticipating gale-force winds when she figures out what I'm up to."

"I hope to God you're right."

"I have to be," he said simply. "Her future, *our* future depends on it."

Harlan Patrick was gone. Laurie came back to the room after taking Amy Lynn for a walk to find her own clothes neatly hung in the closet and his gone. Val watched as she made the discovery, her expression uneasy.

"What do you know about this?" she demanded.

"About what?" Val asked.

"About Harlan Patrick leaving? Did he leave a note?"

"No. He said you'd be hearing from him, though."

"Oh," Laurie said, wearily. "I suppose he got tired of my moping around here. I can't say that I blame him. I just don't seem to have the energy to do anything anymore."

"Then it's a good thing that there's only one more concert to do. You'll be able to get down to Texas and get some rest."

"I don't think I'll be going to Texas, after all," Laurie said. "There doesn't seem to be much point to it now."

Val looked as if she wanted to argue with her, but she said only, "Well, Nick will be happy to hear about the change in plans. He's anxious to see you. He's been worried about you."

"Why?"

Val hesitated. "The reviews haven't been what he hoped for the last couple of cities. You know Nick—he starts imagining that the sky is falling."

She couldn't seem to make herself care about it. "I was off a couple of nights. I know that," she admitted. "I'll do better tonight, I'm sure."

"I'm sure you will, too," Val enthused. "You always knock 'em right out of their seats at the final concert on a tour."

But somehow Laurie couldn't work up any enthusiasm for that final show. She knew that she was letting the audience down. She even apologized for it, but there was no mistaking the sense of disappointment that pervaded the concert hall at the end of the evening. The posttour celebration at the hotel fizzled out when not one of the band members could bear to look her in the eye.

"I'm sorry," she said, and fled.

Upstairs as she approached her room a man stepped out of the shadows.

"Laurie Jensen?"

It was less a question than a statement. There wasn't even time to panic before he was slapping an envelope into her hands and heading for the elevator.

"Wait! What is this?" she called after him, but he was already stepping on the elevator.

Her hand shook as she tried to get her key into the lock. Inside the room, Val was curled up on the sofa, chatting quietly on the phone. When she saw Laurie, she murmured something and hung up.

"What's that?" she asked, spotting the papers in Laurie's hand.

"I'm not sure. A man in the hallway handed them to me, then vanished."

"Legal papers?" Val suggested.

Laurie stared at the envelope. "Legal papers? What kind of legal papers would I be getting?"

"There's only one way to find out."

"Yes, I suppose you're right," Laurie agreed, but her fingers shook as she tried to rip open the envelope.

She unfolded the thick sheaf of papers and began to read. After the first few sentences, the words began to blur.

"No," she whispered, and sank down on the sofa. The papers fell to the floor. "He can't do this. He can't."

"Who can't do what?"

"Harlan Patrick," she said bleakly. "He's suing me for custody of Amy Lynn."

"Can he do that?" Val asked, her expression shocked.

"Well, of course he can. He's an Adams, isn't he?" She shot back to her feet and began to pace. "But he's not going to get away with it—I can tell you that. If he thinks he's going to steal my baby away from me, he's out of his mind."

"You're going to fight him, then?"

She stared at her assistant. "Well, of course I'm going to fight him. Get on the phone and make arrangements for me to get to Texas first thing in the morning. Harlan Patrick isn't going to get away with this. He might be rich and powerful, but I'm Amy Lynn's mother and I've got rights. I've got a little money and influence of my own, by God. I'm a match for any Adams."

"Of course you are," Val soothed.

She turned away, but not before Laurie detected the beginnings of a smile. "What are you grinning about?"

"Nothing."

"Val?"

"Nothing."

"Do you know something about this?"

"Of course not. Harlan Patrick doesn't confide in me."

"Oh, really," Laurie said wryly. "You two certainly had your heads together often enough."

"Not about this," Val insisted.

"Well, I hope you're telling me the truth, because if you're not, you can kiss this job goodbye."

Val did grin at that. "In the meantime I'll make the reservations."

"Forget reservations. Charter a damned plane."

Laurie listened as Val called and booked a charter flight for three. "I gather you're coming along," she said when Val had hung up.

"Are you kidding? I wouldn't miss this for the world."

Laurie was so furious, so terrified, she had Amy Lynn and Val up at dawn and at the airport by seven. A few hours later they were in Los Piños with a rental car waiting at the local airstrip.

"Are we going by your mom's?" Val asked.

"No," Laurie said, aiming straight for White Pines. "You wanted to be in the thick of things, didn't you? Well, strap on your seat belt, honey, 'cause it's gonna get downright bumpy.''

As if to emphasize the point, she hit a bump in the road that just about bounced them through the roof. She still hadn't calmed down by the time they reached the ranch.

Still, her manners hadn't completely deserted her. She managed to make small talk with Melissa and Cody Adams as she deposited Amy Lynn with them and finally shuttled Val off in search of Slade Sutton. She noted that it didn't take much urging to get her assistant to go, despite her protestations that she was here to watch the fireworks.

''Where is he?'' she demanded, her gaze fixed on Cody.

''Harlan Patrick?'' he inquired innocently.

''No, the blasted tooth fairy. Where is he?''

''I believe he's working on his house.''

''Building a new addition,'' Melissa chimed in.

It wasn't until she was climbing the hill to Harlan Patrick's house that the significance of Melissa's words began to sink in. He was building a room for his daughter, in anticipation of gaining custody of her. The sneaky, conniving devil. She wondered if she could bring the whole thing tumbling down and prayed for the chance to try.

She heard the hammering first, then spotted a bare-chested Harlan Patrick on the roof. Good, it would be a nice long drop from up there when she clobbered him. She found the ladder around back and climbed up, nimbly scrambling over the roof until she could stare him in the face. The bare expanse of gleaming chest made it difficult to concentrate, but she forced herself.

"How could you do this?" she demanded.

He glanced up as if he'd just noticed her arrival, which had to be a crock since he had a 360-degree view of the surrounding area from up here.

"Hey, Laurie. What brings you by?"

"Don't you put on that innocent act for me, Harlan Patrick Adams. What the hell do you think you're doing?"

"Building an addition to my house."

She grabbed the hammer out of his hand, only barely resisting the urge to use it to pound some sense into his thick skull.

"I am not talking about right this second, you idiot. I am talking about those papers you had served last night."

He feigned sudden understanding. "Ah, those."

"Yes, those. What were you thinking?"

He shrugged. "I couldn't see any other way to get your attention."

"Oh, you have my attention, all right. I'm so mad I could tear you limb from limb right now."

He grinned. "I can see that."

"Don't you dare laugh at me. This is important, Harlan Patrick. Amy Lynn's future is not some game."

His expression sobered at once. "No, it's not a game," he agreed.

"Then why did you do it? Why did you file for custody?"

"Because I want her here with me. I don't want

her to ever have the same doubts about her daddy's love that you've had about yours." He reached over and tucked a stray curl behind her ear. "I want you here, too, Laurie. Always have."

She'd heard the words before, but for some reason they seemed to take her by surprise. She studied him with bemusement. "Is this your peculiar idea of a proposal, then?"

"That depends."

"On?"

"What you intend to do with that hammer." He gestured toward the tool she was thumping repeatedly into the palm of her hand.

"This?" She paused thoughtfully. "I'm tempted to use it to get your attention."

"How about kissing me instead?" he suggested with a wicked gleam in his eyes.

Before she could respond, he leaned over and took her mouth with an urgency that left her breathless and reeling. She clasped his shoulders to steady herself. That was a mistake, because his skin burned beneath her touch, sending shock waves of desire cascading through her.

She sighed when he released her. "Harlan Patrick, that's never been the problem between us. That's what muddies the waters."

He gazed into her eyes. "Be honest with me, Laurie. Can you do that?"

Something told her that she didn't have a choice. Whatever she said now was going to make all the difference in how the future turned out.

"I'll tell you whatever you want to know," she agreed.

"How do you feel right now?"

"Besides panicked?"

His smile was grim. "Besides that. Being back here, how does it make you feel?"

"I love it here. You know that. I just can't *stay* here."

"Could you stay here some of the time, say, between concert tours and recording sessions?"

Her gaze locked with his, and her heart began to pound. "What are you suggesting?"

"Something I should have insisted on long ago. It's a genuine compromise, darlin'. It's hardly any wonder that neither of us recognize it. Bottom line, we make this our home. You go to Nashville when you need to, go on tour when you have to, but you come back here. Amy Lynn and I'll be waiting and maybe a few more kids when we can fit the baby-making into your busy schedule."

She searched his face, desperate to see if he could truly live with this solution. "Are you sure? Can you really accept having a part-time wife?"

"As long as it's you," he assured her. "It took me long enough to grasp the truth, but I figure having you half the time will be better than having a poor substitute all the time."

She grinned at him. "Harlan Patrick, you do have a romantic way with words."

"I'm not the wordsmith in the family. You are."

"You know," she said slyly, "you can carry a

tune pretty good for a cowboy. Maybe you could come along and sing with me once in a while.''

''No way, darlin'. The bright lights and glamour are all yours.''

Suddenly it all fell into place for her. She had no idea why she'd fought him so long. This was where she belonged, right here, in Harlan Patrick's arms. He'd been steadfast in his love practically forever. Unlike her father, he knew his own heart and was willing to make whatever sacrifices were necessary to keep her in his life.

As for her singing, the acclaim, well, it was all just icing on the cake. He was offering her the chance to have that cake and eat it, too. How could she possibly say no to that when it was what she'd dreamed of practically forever.

''This room you're building, is it going to be a nursery?''

He shook his head. ''A whole new master-bedroom suite with a music room right alongside it, so you can write your songs and rehearse right here at home.''

''Really?''

''Yes. You see, I've been counting on you coming home.''

''Just how far along is this room?''

He grinned. ''Not far enough along for what you've got in mind, but it will be by the time we say I do.''

Laurie looked into his eyes and saw the love there, understood finally the risk he had taken to bring her back from despair. He knew her inside and out and he wanted her.

"I love you, Harlan Patrick Adams."

"I know that."

"I always have."

"I know that, too."

"And you?"

"Darlin', you and our family and White Pines are all I'll ever need to make me a happy man."

She threw her arms around him then, recklessly wrapped her legs around his waist, regardless of their precarious perch on the roof. After all, she was a woman who liked to live dangerously.

"Then prepare yourself to be ecstatic, cowboy," she said, her gaze locked with his. "I'm coming home."

*   *   *   *   *

Watch for Val's story,
as she takes on a very reluctant ex-rodeo star
and his tomboy daughter, in
SUDDENLY, ANNIE'S FATHER
Coming soon from Silhouette books.

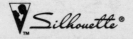

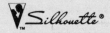

This March Silhouette is proud to present

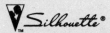 *Silhouette*®

SENSATIONAL

MAGGIE SHAYNE
BARBARA BOSWELL
SUSAN MALLERY
MARIE FERRARELLA

This is a special collection of four complete novels for one low price, featuring a novel from each line: Silhouette Intimate Moments, Silhouette Desire, Silhouette Special Edition and Silhouette Romance.

Available at your favorite retail outlet.

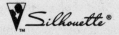 *Silhouette*®

Silhouette® SPECIAL EDITION®

AND BABY MAKES THREE: THE NEXT GENERATION:

The Adams men and women of Texas all find love—and parenthood—in the most unexpected ways!

Bestselling author Sherryl Woods continues to captivate with her popular series about the headstrong heroes and independent-minded ladies of charming Los Pinos, Texas:

November 1998: THE COWGIRL & THE UNEXPECTED WEDDING (SE #1208)

Could fit-to-be-tied cowboy Hank Robbins convince mule-headed mother-to-be Lizzie Adams to march down the aisle?

December 1998: NATURAL BORN LAWMAN (SE #1216)

Justin Adams was a strictly by-the-book lawman—until he fell in love with a desperate, devoted single mom on the run!

February 1999: THE UNCLAIMED BABY
(Silhouette Single Title)

The family saga continues with a passionate, longer-length romance about a fateful stormy night that changes Sharon Adams's life—forever!

March 1999: THE COWBOY AND HIS WAYWARD BRIDE (SE #1234)

Rancher Harlan Patrick Adams would do just about anything to claim stubborn Laurie Jensen—mother of his infant daughter—as his own!

Available at your favorite retail outlet.

SSEBM33

Silhouette®

SPECIAL EDITION®

COMING NEXT MONTH

#1237 A FATHER FOR HER BABY—Celeste Hamilton
That's My Baby!
When Jarrett McMullen saw Ashley Grant again, the sweet beauty he'd once loved and let go was pregnant—and alone. And though the amnesiac mother-to-be couldn't remember her past, Jarrett was determined to claim a place in her future—as the father of her child....

#1238 WRANGLER—Myrna Temte
Hearts of Wyoming
Horse wrangler Lori Jones knew she'd better steer clear of Sunshine Gap's ruggedly appealing deputy sheriff, Zack McBride, who was close to discovering her darkest secret. But then the sexy lawman took her boy under his wing—and made a lasting impression on Lori's wary heart!

#1239 BUCHANAN'S BRIDE—Pamela Toth
Buckles & Broncos
He was lost and alone...but not for long. As luck would have it, feisty cowgirl Leah Randall rescued the stranded stranger, tenderly took him in and gave him all her love. But would their blossoming romance survive the revelation that this dynamic man was a long-lost relation of her sworn enemy?

#1240 FINALLY HIS BRIDE—Christine Flynn
The Whitaker Brides
After nearly a decade, Trevor Whitaker still left Erin Gray breathless. Their bittersweet reunion brought back memories of unfulfilled passion—and broken promises. But her ardor for this devastatingly handsome man was intoxicating. Would Erin's fantasy of being a Whitaker bride finally come true?

#1241 A WEDDING FOR MAGGIE—Allison Leigh
Men of the Double-C Ranch
When Daniel Clay returned to the Double-C ranch, the tormented cowboy knew he was unworthy of his beloved Maggie. But when their night of love left Maggie pregnant, Daniel stubbornly insisted on a convenient union. But then a headstrong Maggie made a marriage demand of her own....

#1242 NOT JUST ANOTHER COWBOY—Carol Finch
Alexa Tipton had her fill of charming rodeo men. So the serious-minded single mom was beside herself when she became irresistibly attracted to the fun-loving Chance Butler. The sexy superstar cowboy began to melt her steely resistance, but could she trust their happiness would last?